Clever & Excellent

2-1-86

NYC

THE RIDE

JOHN WAINWRIGHT
THE RIDE

St. Martin's Press
New York

Library of Congress Cataloging in Publication Data

Wainwright, John William, 1921-
  The ride.

I. Title.
PR6073.A354R5   1984   823'.914   84-22854
ISBN 0-312-68229-8

First published in Great Britain by Macmillan London Ltd.

First U.S. Edition

10 9 8 7 6 5 4 3 2 1

ONE

Murders are messy. Some, of course, are more messy than others; smother the victim with a pillow, strangle him with piano wire, use arsenic instead of castor sugar on his sponge cake and unless, as sometimes happens, the bowels and the bladder empty themselves when he gives up the ghost, you have a non-messy murder. Comparatively non-messy. But blast off at him with a shotgun, slice his windpipe with a sharp knife or bash his skull in with a blunt instrument and you have mess all over the place. Gallons of it. If the killing takes place in a room the carpets and furnishings are saturated in gore. Great streaks and gobs of the stuff pattern the walls. It even splashes the ceiling. And not only blood. Brain tissue, slivers of shattered bone, multi-coloured mucus and membrane. All the general goo that biology masters talk about, but rarely put on show. This time it's *all* on show!

And when Clive Richardson got his, it was a *very* messy murder.

Seven days ago, when his daily cleaning woman had opened the bedroom door to deliver his morning cup of pre-breakfast coffee, she'd seen the mess and promptly fainted. Then she'd come round long enough to call the police before fainting again.

Since then it had been all go. Door-to-door questioning, long sessions with his friends and acquaintances, forensic science jiggery-pokery, post mortem prodding and probing, statements by the hundred, computer run-throughs . . . and the result?

A very select few could put a name to the murderer.

Detective Constable Bill Mathews was not one of that select few. He and P.C. Clarke had been working in double-harness since the start of the enquiry, and Bill Mathews was feeling his age. House-to-house enquiries looked good on paper, but seven days of it was going some. A blazing July (one of the hottest on record), warm, hard pavements and a prickly-heat rash at the crotch and under the arms which no amount of showers and camomile lotion would shift. Policing! Four years to Pension Day, mate – four short years – and then they could stuff it. Let the mad bastards run riot. Let 'em lift everything, from the Crown Jewels down. See if he'd care. What? A little place on the west coast, somewhere. Feet up in winter, pottering around in the garden in summer. A promise – a promise he'd made to himself long ago – he'd draw pension for as many years as he'd shafted at the job. *He'd* see to that. He'd have his pound of flesh. By Christ he would. Best rump steak . . . with trimmings.

He turned into one of the tiny 'gardens of rest' which dotted Hallsworth Hill Division and flopped down on a form. Clarke followed and joined him.

Jim Clarke. A quiet lad; less than five years in uniform, but liked and already making something of a name for himself as one you could trust; an introvert, maybe, but what of that? Just the stuff for this new-fangled Community Policing lark. This was his beat. A sort of village bobby responsible for one patch of streets, shops and offices within the sprawling complex of Lessford City. Maybe it would work. If so, men like Jim Clarke would *make* it work.

Clarke smiled and said, 'Tired?'

'Knackered,' said Mathews.

'My first murder enquiry,' mused Clarke. 'I didn't think

it would be like this.'

'Every one different.' Mathews leaned forward and untied his shoe laces in order to give his feet a little more air. 'The old lass shoves the carving knife into her husband. We arrive . . . she's still there holding the knife. It's murder.'

'Motiveless?' Clarke sounded mildly surprised.

'Not really. He's grumbled once too often. Twenty, thirty years of griping. It's the only way she can stop his rattle.'

'You've known that?'

'And dafter.' Mathews nodded. 'Couldn't agree which television programme to watch.'

'No!'

'It's a fact. *My* first. ITV, BBC. Each wanted to watch the other side. He ended the argument by pushing her, head first, through the screen.'

'Good God!'

'It's not the big things, old son.' Mathews eased a foot from its shoe and began to massage his toes. 'Little things. Potty things that go on, year after year.' He grinned. 'My old lass. We both like an open fire, but she *will* light the bloody thing with today's newspaper . . . and before I've even seen the headlines. I'll swing for her yet.'

'So why was Richardson killed?' asked Clarke tentatively.

'He was a poofty.' Mathews made the statement with solemn, but puzzled, overtones. 'Chances are by another poofty.' Then, hurriedly, 'Don't get me wrong, lad. I don't understand 'em, but at the same time I don't condemn 'em. Not out of hand. They're . . . *different*. That's all.'

'Different motives?'

'I wouldn't know.' Mathews eased his foot back into its shoe. 'Those I've known – the few I've *known* to be gay – good and bad, like the rest of us.' He bent to re-tie the laces. 'But, extreme . . . see? The good, very good. Couldn't wish for nicer blokes. But the bad. No half measures. Real

7

bastards.'

They left the bench and continued the house-to-house stuff. A waste of time and they both knew it. The same questions, the same negative answers over and over again. It filled in the day, and it looked good when the HMI visited and asked to see the Murder File. Bobbying! Just about the most crazy way of all to earn a living.

'If,' said Flensing, 'we pull him in, he has to *stay* in. No Yorkshire Ripper game of yo-yo. Into a cell, up in a dock, and from there behind granite.'

'We daren't risk it,' observed Hoyle.

'Not now,' agreed Flensing. 'Not at this particular moment. We lack the evidence. So, let him feel "safe". It's a cat-and-mouse game, David. The Express Message is out to all forces. We're busy "pursuing enquiries". The motions, my young friend. The impression of a force that doesn't know which way to turn. That's what he'll think. That's what we *want* him to think.'

Flensing. Detective Chief Superintendent Flensing, Head of Lessford Regional C.I.D. The final can-catcher in a police area of some considerable size. A man literally married to his job because, in the true sense, he couldn't be married to a wife imprisoned in an iron lung. A man whose voice was rarely more than a quiet drawl; who never seemed to hurry but, via some personal magic, always arrived first. He'd been tested and tried; measured against the legendary Sullivan, and not found wanting. Figuratively speaking he was the sabre, where Sullivan might have been likened to the butcher's cleaver. Each as deadly as the other. Each equally capable of hacking a path to reach the man they were after.

And Hoyle. Detective Chief Inspector David Hoyle, and rather more than Flensing's second-in-command. Flensing's friend, if only because Hoyle's wife worked part-time in the hospital where Helen Flensing reluctantly watched a very small world through a mirror. The two women had become deeply attached to each other; they shared secrets; their mutual affection was deeper than that between many sisters. Ralph Flensing appreciated the bond and, because Hoyle was also a damn good copper, they too had become more than colleagues.

'A cough.' Hoyle lighted a cigarette as he spoke the word, then held out the packet to Flensing. 'The cough to end all coughs. That's what we really need.'

'That, plus a Guilty plea.' Flensing took a cigarette and held the end in the flame of Hoyle's lighter. 'We need a Guilty plea. If we don't get that, and he retracts the statement, we're back at the start-line. Worse. He'll walk away, and we won't be able to charge him again.'

'Which means?' Hoyle raised questioning eyebrows.

'A set-up,' said Flensing calmly. 'A con that doesn't *look* like a con. A con that lasts all through the trial and until he's sent down. Something special.'

'Illegal?' Hoyle frowned his disapproval.

'Not illegal. Unusual.'

They were in Flensing's office at Lessford Regional Headquarters. Flensing pushed himself from the desk chair and strolled to a wall which held glass-fronted book-shelves from floor to ceiling. The shelves were filled with books, and all the books were related to Criminal Law.

'Harris and Wilshere. Stone's. Kenney's. Gregg. Clarke. Even Moriarty.' He tapped the glass gently with a knuckle as he named the various standard textbooks. He turned to face Hoyle. 'The whole lot of them. Your Bibles, David. None of them written by a street copper. They all tell you what to do. Not one of them tells you how the hell to do it.' Then, as Hoyle made as if to object, 'I know . . . they preach perfection and you're a perfectionist. That's fine as far as it goes. But don't turn perfection into a trip-wire. Stay within the law, certainly, but let's play it like *they* play it. They look for holes in the law. Ways round the law. If

9

they can, *we* can. Something the pundits haven't latched onto. That's what I'm after.' As he wandered back to the desk chair he continued, 'I think I have it. The broad generalities. Nobody gets hurt, and a criminal ends up where he belongs. Any objections?'

'No, sir.' The reply had a certain stiffness to it.

'Not illegal, David.' Flensing smiled. 'A little unusual . . . that's all.'

As far as Belamy was concerned, none of the books in Flensing's office need have been written. When the occasion warranted it, Belamy could be a one-man Panzer division. Belamy was a detective sergeant, and he'd been taught bobbying by his father, who'd been a uniformed sergeant, and Belamy honoured his father and remembered every word of paternal wisdom. 'It's us versus them, Dick. Never forget that. Give the sods half a chance, they'll screw you into the ground left-hand thread.'

People were frightened of Detective Sergeant Belamy. And not just jail-fodder. Fellow-coppers didn't line up to work alongside this one. It was a dangerous occupation. When Belamy leaned you could use the tower of Pisa as a plumb-line and his tact was on a par with that of an enraged fighting bull. Nine times he'd been carpeted; nine Misconduct Sheets, and each time he'd had his balls well and truly roasted by Gilliant, the chief constable. But he still remained a detective sergeant. Not a hope in hell of promotion, but at the same time not so much as a hint of *de*motion. And why: Because he delivered the rashers. He could take the ballockings. Ballockings went with the job if, by Belamy's yardstick, you felt the collars you were paid to feel. The bent bastards might rule the world . . . but they didn't rule *his* world.

And Belamy, too, was on house-to-house. In the centre of Lessford, and well away from the scene of the crime. He was, as usual, working solo and he was 'questioning' one of the assistants in a male outfitters.

'You're one of the bum brigade,' he said bluntly. 'So was Richardson. You're all in the same clique.'

'I – I . . .'

The assistant looked a little wildly around the poky office which the branch manager had placed at Belamy's disposal.

'It's not illegal,' he whispered.

'No,' agreed Belamy. 'Neither is chewing barbed wire. It's just a thing most people don't do.'

'Being gay isn't a . . .'

'Don't use that bloody word,' snapped Belamy. 'You're a poofty. An arse-bandit. So was Richardson.'

'I – I don't see what . . .'

'Because *I* think he was killed by one of his kind.'

'Oh!'

'That's why I'm here.'

'For God's sake! You don't think *I* . . .'

'I don't know. Tell me.'

'We – we were *friends.*'

'Big deal.'

'I – I don't know what to say,' moaned the assistant.

'Think of something.' Belamy raised a hand and pushed the assistant on the chest. The assistant staggered back, caught the back of his knees against a chair and sat down. The chair teetered for a moment then righted itself. As he lowered himself onto the only other chair in the miniature office, Belamy said, 'Take the weight off your feet, sonny, and think. Start by thinking of Richardson.'

'What? I mean . . . what about Richardson?'

'He's dead. He's where all good little poofties go when they leave this world.'

'I – I know that. But . . .'

'He was hurried on his way.'

'Look, I know . . .'

'Who by?'

11

The assistant gaped.

'You?' suggested Belamy calmly.

'Good God! You don't seriously think . . .'

'Can you prove it *wasn't* you?'

'I – I don't know. How do I . . .'

'Because we just might be able to prove it *was*.'

'Eh!'

'Time, day and date . . . y'know. Blood group. Finger-prints. We're not mugs, sonny. We've been this way before.'

'*I didn't kill him.*' The assistant almost screamed the words.

'No?' Belamy sounded quite surprised.

'You know damn well . . .'

'Oh, no.' Belamy shook his head. 'I know very little. That's why I'm here. To find out.'

'I was nowhere near his place.'

'No? Where were you?'

'At a . . .' The assistant swallowed. 'At a party.'

'Birthday party?'

'Er – yes.' After the first hesitation, the answer was too pat.

'Whose?'

'I'd rather not say.'

'Do you think you have a choice?' Belamy sounded mildly interested.

'I – I don't suppose so,' groaned the assistant. Then, 'It wasn't actually a *birthday* party.'

'No?'

'Just – just a party. Y'know . . . a party.'

'A dinner party,' suggested Belamy.

'Yes. More or less.'

'Much more? Or much less?'

'I – I beg your pardon?'

'Don't let's play mulberry bush.' Belamy's voice had a distinct edge. 'The hell it was a dinner party, any more

12

than it was a birthday party. What sort of party was it?'

'We – we watched films,' gulped the assistant.

'Porn?'

The assistant nodded.

'Who was there? And don't tell me you don't know or can't remember. For sure it wasn't at the local Odeon, so there'd be a very limited audience. Where, sonny? And who was getting cheap thrills?'

And, be it understood, this was a very pianissimo going over by Belamy's standards. The assistant mopped his sweating face a couple of times with his handkerchief, but within thirty minutes Belamy had names and addresses. All homosexuals; male and female. And Richardson wasn't one of them.

As he stood up from the chair, Belamy said, 'If I find you've been feeding me glorified garbage . . .' He left the sentence unfinished.

'No. It's the truth. Honestly, sergeant.' Then in a tremulous tone, 'What – what about my job?'

'Here?'

'Yes. I mean . . .'

'I don't start and sack, sonny. The manager says you're a good worker. This little get-together doesn't concern him. I'll mention you've been a big help. No more.'

'Thanks.' The assistant gulped his gratitude. 'Thank you very much, sergeant.'

'As you say,' growled Belamy, 'it's not illegal any more.'

The day drew to a sticky, sweaty close. Kids on roller-skates tried the patience of pavement pedestrians. The bourgeoisie trundled their mowers over the scorched grass of their lawns or dead-headed roses which should have been still in full flower. In the parks the bowling greens, putting greens and tennis courts were booked solid for the rest of the evening. God, it was hot!

It was hot in the Murder Room. *The Murder Room*, you

understand. A hand-printed sign Sellotaped to the door named it as such. Flensing tended to call a spade a spade, and would have none of this new-fangled phraseology. It was not an 'Incident Centre'. It was a room, earmarked as the eye of the hurricane, and the hurricane was the upsurge of police activity following the unlawful killing of a human being. Murder. Ergo, it was a *Murder* Room.

People came and went. They didn't stay long; it was too damn hot. They passed on what snippets of information they'd gathered, the clerks noted those snippets of information . . . then back to the street again, where it was a few degrees cooler. The typists hammered away at their machines. They were stripped as far as official decency would allow, but despite this they had to keep flicking the perspiration from their eyes as it dripped from their brows. The clerks collected the cards from the out trays, referenced them and cross-referenced them, then tucked them away in the filing cabinets.

The part of a man-hunt the public rarely sees. The sheer mass of forms and indices. And it *must* be controlled. The snowball effect is such that the end-product can result in indexes *for* indexes, while somewhere, hidden in this Everest of paper, *the* name or *the* clue is lost for ever. The emphasis is on filing, and not on searching. The enquiry becomes more important than the result of the enquiry. It happens. It is a little like feeding sand into a ball-race; what should run smoothly grinds to a horrible halt, and nothing on God's earth can shift it. And the harder you work – the more paper you produce in an attempt to get the damn thing moving again – the firmer it becomes.

The sergeant clerk in charge of the Murder Room was no fool. He knew the danger, and despite the heat he moved around, checking and re-checking. 'No more than three verifications of any fact. Pick the three best. Sling the others to one side as possible back-ups, but don't include them in the main file.' He kept everybody on their toes. It didn't

14

make for popularity, but what the hell? 'Look, this guy. Four people – independent, decent people – give him a clean bill. Okay, he was a possible. Even a suspect. Now he *isn't*. Don't clutter up the damn filing cabinets with names of people we know *didn't* murder Richardson.'

A line of soap-box cartons lined one wall of the room. The discarded statement and index cards weren't destroyed – you could never be *absolutely* sure – but instead they were tossed into the cartons and, in effect, forgotten.

Flensing called at the Murder Room prior to going off duty for a spell. The conversation was between Flensing and the sergeant clerk.

'Movement?' asked Flensing, with a smile.

'If there is, I haven't noticed it.'

'It'll come with a rush.' Flensing ran a finger around the inside of his collar. 'God, it's hot in here.'

'We have every window open, sir.'

'Get some fans. Contact Headquarter Stores. Half a dozen fans.'

'Will they *have* fans?' The sergeant clerk sounded doubtful.

'If not ring round the divisions. If necessary buy some. Send the bill into Accounts . . . I'll see it gets paid.'

'Yes, sir.'

'Anybody fainted yet?' asked Flensing.

'Not yet.'

'Fine. Spell everybody in rotation. Fifteen minutes break, one at a time.'

'Thank you, sir.'

'And that includes yourself.'

The sergeant clerk nodded. Flensing was *his* man; a fine copper who knew how to drive, but also knew how to get the most out of his men.

Flensing said, 'I'm going off for a few hours. Home number till about eight. After that, the hospital.'

'Yes, sir.'

15

Lessford was a city and, like every other city, it was made up of a mish-mash of groups, sects, communities, oddballs, enthusiasts, believers, non-believers and general followers. They sported every shade of skin from pearly white through bronze to the shiny blackness of good coal. Name a religion and it was catered for – plus a handful few people had ever heard of. Politically, its inhabitants ranged from lunatic Red up (or down, as the case may be) to rampant neo-Nazi.

It was a city.

It had its homosexuals; male and female. Discounting the 'closet queens', the gay community of Lessford numbered well over a hundred, all of whom were openly gay and made no secret of it. They favoured the one club-cum-disco, The Callboy, but mainly because the manager was one of their number. He ran a cheerful, value-for-money establishment and, in the language of the day, A/C and D/C mixed without aggro.

The manager and five of his fellows were in a side room of the club, discussing the recent mild harassment by the police.

One of the more outraged said, 'It's not good enough. Why us?'

A second man said, 'Clive was one of us. That's why.'

A third man contributed, 'That's no reason. We don't commit murder anymore than the straight crowd.'

The outraged one said, 'I think we should complain to the chief constable. We're being discriminated against. We're being bloody hounded.'

The manager chuckled and said, 'That's a bit strong, boy. I'll answer questions. Why not? I want the bastard caught . . . whoever he is.'

The second man said, 'Writing to the chief constable won't do any good. He'll back Flensing.'

'Flensing's okay. It's that Belamy bastard I object to.'

'It's his way, boy.'

'I don't *like* his way.'

'Look,' pleaded the manager, 'we're accepted. The few who *don't* accept us aren't worth worrying about . . .'

'Sure, but maybe one of *them* did it.'

'. . . so don't rock the boat. It's a civilised town. Let's not make agony for ourselves by being stupid.'

'I'll go along with that. Just that they get who killed poor old Clive.'

Five of them agreed wholeheartedly with the last remark . . . but one of them didn't.

Detective Chief Superintendent Ralph Flensing walked the corridors of the hospital. He knew his way; knew which room he was making for. It was a near-daily pilgrimage, and it was the one moment of the day he lived for.

Had you asked more than half the coppers in the division they might have told you he was an unmarried man. Single. Divorced. A widower. Something of that sort. Only Hoyle had ever seen his wife, and Hoyle kept his own council.

The truth was, Flensing's life was divided into two separate compartments. The copper and the husband. The two didn't mix. The two *couldn't* mix. He'd married a good woman. He'd said 'For better or for worse' and, unlike a goodly percentage of men, he'd *meant* it. 'Sickness and health'. 'Till death us do part'. Oaths made before an altar. And she'd made similar oaths.

Not that Flensing was over-religious. He 'believed', but what it *was* he believed stumped him. Gentle Jesus, meek and mild. Big deal! But there'd been nothing gentle – nothing either meek or mild – in the way those young tearaways had made a getaway from an abortive smash-and-grab in a stolen car; mounted the pavement and dragged his wife between the car and a wall, smashed her to hell and forced her to live nine-tenths of the rest of her life in a stainless steel cylinder. *And* they'd got away with it.

Oh, he'd prayed. For a full fourteen days he'd prayed.

17

Not just at night, not just in the morning and not even on his knees. But he'd prayed all right. Prayed, and at the same time raged at God. To *her*. Why in hell to *her*? She'd done nothing wrong, done no evil, and yet . . . While the surgeons fought for her life, Flensing had prayed. Fear, perhaps. But more than fear. A knowledge that, without her, he was no damn good. Without her, *he* was as good as dead. Not the Our Father bit. That didn't mean a thing. That didn't take into account mindless bastards who could pulp an innocent woman between a car and a wall and not even slow down. Just a pact. A pact between Flensing and God. 'Let her live. Anything . . . just let her live.'

The prayer had been answered, therefore he 'believed'. Somebody had heard him, somebody had given those surgeons that extra skill . . . okay, he accepted the rest, without complaint. His prayers had been answered.

He opened the door of the tiny ward, saw her and smiled. A real, genuine smile of happiness. Not a put-on. A smile that almost amounted to a grin of sheer delight.

He closed the door, and said, 'You're lucky.'

She turned her head on the pillow. Just her head. The rest of her was hidden in the contraption necessary to keep her breathing.

He said, 'In here, it's cool. Out there, you could fry eggs on the pavement.'

He reached her, stroked the white hair gently then bent to kiss her on the lips. Again, not a put-on. That kiss was a kiss; no mere touching of lips; there was carnality there, even though it was the only carnality they could ever know.

'Ralph.' She returned the smile. As genuine and as real as his own.

He pulled a chair nearer to her head and sat down.

'What's new?' he asked.

'I have a new boy friend,' she chuckled.

'Should I be jealous?'

'Of course.'

18

'Okay, I'm jealous.'

'The ward sister brought her nephew in to see me. Two years old.' She gave a single nod at the angled mirror above her head. 'That looking-glass thing fascinated him. He thought I'd two heads.'

'We'll have to find a side-show.'

'A super kid.' Sadness touched her tone. 'I read Rupert Bear to him for more than an hour.'

'Thank her for me.' And, this time, *his* voice was sombre.

'Ralph . . .' she began.

'Don't say it.'

'Why not?'

'I don't want to hear it.'

'You don't even know what I was going to say.'

'I want *you*, not kids.' There was almost violence in the remark.

'You have neither,' she said gently.

'I thought we'd got over this bit,' he growled.

'Will we ever . . . really?'

'I have. I never had it.'

'You're a good man, Ralph. A fine man.'

'Ask some of the villains I've put away.'

'Don't!' she pleaded.

'Sweetheart.' He stroked her cheek with the back of his fingers. 'You think too much. You worry too much. I'm fine. I'm happy. I wish you'd let yourself be as happy.'

'In this damn thing?'

'Easy, sweetheart,' he murmured. 'Take it easy. We're luckier than some people.'

'Who, for instance?'

'Lighthouse keepers,' he smiled. 'We see each other just about every day.'

'Don't make silly excuses, Ralph.'

'I don't think they're silly.'

'Dammit, you're a man.' The frustration of her imprisonment in the iron lung made her moods fluctuate wildly.

19

Flensing knew this and allowed the upsurge of rage to run its course. She stormed, 'You need a woman. You need a *wife*. Not something like this . . . like me. You have emotions, like other men. You need to make love. Not *this*.'

'It's much over-rated,' drawled Flensing mildly.

'What is?'

'Copulation. With you it was different. Special.'

'Don't make . . .'

'I'm not making excuses.' His tone hardened very slightly. 'You think I'd go for second best when I've experienced the best?'

'I'm no good to you.' And now she wasn't far from tears.

'Not if you start blubbing you aren't.'

'Ralph, please don't . . .'

'No!' He took a deep breath. 'Subject closed. Finished. Done with.'

'You're not talking to your . . .'

'I'm talking to you. And *you're* the one who said "obey". Now . . . *end it*. You can't make me visit. I don't visit out of sympathy. I visit because you're my wife and I'm still crazy about you. That's it. That's all there is to it. Now, *be* a wife . . . and don't call your husband a liar without proof.'

He stood up from the chair and wandered aimlessly around the tiny ward. He had wisdom. Wisdom and love. He understood; knew what she was feeling and what she was thinking. Why not? Wouldn't he? Wouldn't *anybody*? He stood by the window and looked out at the tarmac car park. At the shimmering heat hovering above the surface.

It was as near as they ever got to arguing. And always the same damn subject. And yet, she *knew*. Deep down, she *knew*. Had the positions been reversed, she'd have been the same, and he'd have been as troubled. They'd had a few years of normality. A few precious years. All they could ask for. Everything they could ask for. Everything *anybody* could ask for. Be satisfied, my love. Remember . . . and give thanks.

He heard the sound of a tissue being used.

Sure he wanted a woman sometimes. Dammit, he was normal. He wanted a woman – yearned for a woman – *one* woman. The woman he couldn't have. A woman locked away in a glorified dustbin. Hell's teeth! Her or nobody.

In a soft, but steady voice, Helen Flensing said, 'Tell me about the case, darling.'

Flensing allowed himself a slow, twisted smile, before he turned. He knew this wife of his. The few moments of self-pity (and that's all it had been) were over. No more spats of ill-temper . . . until next time. They'd come again. Of course they would. But rarely and understandable. A small price to pay for what she'd given him, and still gave him.

He returned to the chair, took her hand and kissed the palm lightly before he spoke.

'The case,' he said gently, 'has reached a brick wall.'

'As bad as that?'

'Oh, no.' He shook his head. 'We know "who". What we lack is proof. There seems to *be* no proof.'

'None?'

'Not enough,' he corrected himself. 'Proof enough for us, but not proof enough for a jury.'

'Tell me,' she invited.

He told her. Everything. She listened with real interest, but he knew she'd keep her council. She was a policeman's wife, and proud of it. She could take secrets, and they'd remain secrets. As far as Flensing was concerned it was a great asset. Some coppers didn't have it; they daren't tell their wives, because their wives couldn't hold confidences. It upset marriages. It had broken marriages. But those who *could* . . . it strengthened the marriage.

He ended, 'We know who he is, we know where he is. He doesn't know it, but he's under surveillance every minute of the day. We can pick him up . . .' He snapped his fingers. 'Just like that.' Then, with a sigh, 'And if we do we'll show our hand, and he'll laugh at us.'

'You could interview him.'

'Of course.' He nodded. 'We could crack him . . . I've no doubt about that. Crack him, get a statement. Then he'd retract his statement – swear it was taken under duress, plead Not Guilty – we'd be back at square one.'

'What's the answer, then?' she asked.

'Make him plead Guilty.'

The murderer sat in a corner of the Plymouth Sound Hotel and enjoyed his beer. Oddly enough, he wasn't a bad man. He'd killed, but that in itself didn't make him *bad*. He'd panicked. As simple as that. But if Richardson had *meant* it, when he'd threatened to expose him . . .

They'd never find him, of course. That was one comfort. A gay gets killed and the police hound all the other gays of that particular city. The way they worked. The way they always worked. The known gays of Lessford would have a rough time, but they'd be okay. There was nothing to link *him*.

Dear God, why had he to be this way? Despite everything, the ordinary man-in-the-street wouldn't accept it. Good men, fine men, even brilliant men were like him. Artists. Musicians. Actors. But always the snigger. Always mentioned in the newspaper. In God's name, *why*?

That was why he'd killed. Just that. Because to *be* a 'queen' meant you *could* be blackmailed. You *could* lose your job. You *could* . . . anything!

He drank his beer and enjoyed it. Cool, refreshing beer. But that's as far as the enjoyment went.

The manager of The Callboy was lucky. He'd left the club-cum-disco in the hands of his sidekick while he visited Lessford Regional H.Q. to lodge a purely unofficial complaint. He was the best spokesman they had and somebody had to tell the cops.

He was lucky in that he almost collided with Detective

22

Chief Inspector Hoyle as that officer hurried down the shallow steps leading to the main entrance of the headquarters building. They knew each other – even respected each other – therefore when the manager called, 'Chief Inspector, can I have a word?' Hoyle stopped and smiled.

They walked alongside each other as Hoyle made his way towards the car park at the rear of the building.

The manager said, 'The Clive Richardson thing.'

'What about it?'

'Just that, I know you have a job to do, but my friends think you're giving them a little too much stick.'

'Your – er – "friends".'

'You know what I mean, sir.'

'The queers?'

'I never expected to hear you use that word, sir.' The manager sounded disappointed.

'Homosexuals,' submitted Hoyle.

'We're human beings,' said the manager quietly.

'So was Richardson.'

'Of course . . . *and* a homosexual.'

'A fellow-homosexual murdered him.'

'You're sure of that?' pressed the manager.

'He was naked and in his bedroom. That suggests – more than suggests – certain things.'

'It made good reading in some of the newspapers,' said the manager bitterly.

'We give the media the facts. How they present those facts is their responsibility.' Nevertheless a hint of apology might have been detected in Hoyle's tone.

'Some of your men are making it hard for us,' insisted the manager. 'I know . . . they're doing their job. It's an easy excuse.'

'A valid excuse.'

'It's the *way* they're doing the job that's upsetting us.'

'Don't you want the killer found?' asked Hoyle mildly.

'Of course. It could have been any of us.'

'Could it?' Hoyle seemed interested in the proposition.

They reached the car – a Cortina – and Hoyle leaned against the wing. He made no move to open the door of the car.

Instead he said, 'Off the record. Tell me about Richardson.'

'He – er . . .' The manager moved a shoulder. 'He was okay.'

'Speak no ill of the dead,' mocked Hoyle softly.

'All right.' The manager seemed to reach a decision. 'He wasn't quite like the rest of us . . . most of us.'

'In what way.'

'You wouldn't understand,' sighed the manager.

'I'll try,' promised Hoyle.

'You're married,' said the manager flatly.

'Happily.' Hoyle nodded.

'So are we . . . most of us.'

Hoyle waited.

The manager continued, 'It's possible, you know. For a man to love another man. For a woman to love another woman. It doesn't *have* to be man and woman.'

'Fine.' Hoyle's tone was gentle. 'I won't insult you by saying I understand. I don't. But I accept your word.'

'It's possible,' repeated the manager. 'Call it a liaison, if you like. It's serious. As serious as any marriage. A man and another man. A woman and another woman. Don't try to understand . . . unless you're one of us, you can't. But the love's there. Love, not lust. And, just occasionally, some clergyman blesses the union. Not a Marriage Service. Nothing like that. But it's for real. As serious – as deep – as your sort of marriage. It needs guts.' A sadness had entered his tone. 'It needs real guts, Mr Hoyle. Nobody laughs at your weddings. Happy laughter, maybe. But not sniggering laughter. Dirty jokes. That's what we get. Snide headlines and blue comedians making filthy jokes. That's because – because . . .'

His voice trailed off.

'Richardson,' said Hoyle gently.

'Oh, yeah . . . Richardson.' The manager gave a deep sigh and seemed to push aside the previous hint of sadness. 'Let's put it this way. Clive was like a whore. Like a cheap tart. Anybody's.' He frowned. 'You'll not understand that, of course.'

'Anybody's,' repeated Hoyle. 'Yes. I understand. No permanent partner . . . that's what you mean.'

'More or less, but more than that.' The manager chewed his lower lip for a moment. 'Y'see, we can't all come out. "Coming out" . . . that's – that's accepting ourselves for what we are. Not being ashamed. Not being secretive. Realising there's more than one yardstick of normality.'

'I know what "Coming out" means,' said Hoyle.

'But those of us who won't . . .' Again, the pause. Again the quick nibble of the lower lip. 'Some men – gays – they *daren't* come out. Different reasons. They're wrong, of course. *I* think they're wrong. But they daren't. Won't. Clive catered for them. He – er – made himself known. That he was – y'know – available.'

'For money?' asked Hoyle.

'I wouldn't know. Maybe. I suppose so . . . sometimes. But that's what Clive Richardson was. The sort we *don't* like.'

'You accepted him,' said Hoyle. 'He was one of *you*.'

'They *all* are.' This time impatience was in the tone. 'We're the *real* minority, Mr Hoyle. People won't accept that. We're "different". For kicks . . . that's what most people believe. We should pull ourselves together. Be decent. Those are the arguments . . . *and they aren't arguments*. They all have a false basis. So we stick together. However much we differ in other things, we're all the same. That! So forget other differences. They're not important. A man – a woman – if they're an open gay they're one of us. Accepted. Whatever else.'

25

'Why tell me all this?' asked Hoyle.

'For the others.' The manager hesitated. 'We think we're being hounded.' Then, hurriedly, before Hoyle could answer the accusation. 'All right, you think Clive was murdered by a homosexual. You're probably right. But not by one of *us*. The analogy again. I'm sorry, sir – I don't mean to be impertinent, but it's the only way I can explain – you're a happily married man, you don't consort with whores, therefore you would have no reason to murder a whore. You see what I'm getting at?'

'Of course.' Hoyle smiled, then added, 'But *I* know *I'm* happily married. I can't speak with any degree of certainty about other men. You see what *I'm* getting at?'

TWO

Fourteen days, and a murder can become old. Even boring. It depends, of course. Child-murder, the murder of some good-looking young woman, with rape as a prelude and, of course, the personality – the charisma – of the man in charge of the enquiry . . . given these things, in combination or abundance, and the killing may leave the headlines, but it will stay on the front page. It will stay fresh and remain news.

But the killing of one unknown homosexual in a provincial city whose inhabitants number almost a million . . . who really cares?

House-to-house enquiries had come to a close. The uniformed boys were back on their beats. The Murder Room had seen little movement for days and the staff had been reduced to an absolute minimum. Most of the jacks were back chasing run-of-the-mill criminals, and the few still on the murder hunt were 'pushing putty' and wishing to hell they, too, could get back to *real* enquiries.

It was, you see, a subtle balancing act. A deliberate marking of time on the part of Flensing (and those very few in the know) in the hope that the murderer might feel safe and, feeling safe, might make the wrong move or say the wrong thing to the wrong person.

It was infuriating, but necessary.

'We don't have enough evidence.' For the umpteenth time Hoyle voiced the complaint in the privacy of

Flensing's office.

'*We* have enough evidence.' Flensing's quick smile was a little weary. 'But the D.P.P. wouldn't agree.'

'Damn!' Hoyle smacked a fist into the palm of his other hand. 'He's made mistakes.'

'Not enough.'

'So what are we left with?'

'A conscience,' said Flensing slowly. 'A conscience and an imagination . . . and our own ability to know *when*.'

Belamy was still on the enquiry, and Belamy hated not getting anywhere. He was, therefore, going to *get* somewhere, who the hell suffered. And the man suffering was starting to bite back.

'All right,' he snapped. 'You can prove things, but be warned. Don't!'

'Or what?'

'I'll leave that to your imagination, sergeant. Just think about it.'

'You've been inside for it,' accused Belamy.

'Twenty years ago.'

'When it was illegal.' Belamy made no effort to hide his disgust that 'it' was no longer illegal. 'You knew Richardson.'

'All right. I knew Richardson. As an acquaintance . . . no more. Damn it, we lived within a hundred yards of each other. He was a neighbour.'

'And more.' Belamy was getting desperate.

'Why me?' The man fought to control himself. As is so often the case, a previous conviction tended towards bringing on an irrational feeling of guilt. The police – especially the C.I.D. – were capable of putting him away. They'd done it once in the past. A long time ago, and then he'd *been* guilty. But there were rumours. Newspaper reports. Common sense insisted that the coppers didn't like an undetected murder on their books. Something had to be done. Something! Or *somebody*. He almost moaned, 'In God's name, why *me*?'

'Why *not* you? Somebody iced him.'

They were in Belamy's car. The man had been walking home from work; he still wore a boiler-suit and on his lap was a tin box in which he carried his lunch. He was worried. Of course he was worried; in his younger days he'd mixed with the wrong crowd, and as a result he'd done things of which he was now ashamed. But that was *years* ago. The spell inside had knocked all the stupidity out of him, and since then he hadn't put a foot wrong.

'You must have dug deep,' he said bitterly.

'We don't stop at the day before yesterday,' growled Belamy.

'Twenty bloody years!'

'And for the rest of your life.'

'Sergeant Belamy, you're an evil man.' The accusation came from the back of the throat. The anger was still there, but it was an anger shot with scorn and, perhaps, carrying a hint of pity. 'What I *am* – what I've worked to become – that doesn't mean a thing. You're not interested. You have a murderer to find.'

'I'll find him.'

'Or invent one.'

'Watch it! I don't take . . .'

'Why should I "watch it"? I'm a married man with two kids. Fine kids and a good wife . . .'

'It's been known.'

'. . . but that doesn't mean a thing. Today doesn't matter. Twenty years ago. That's all *you're* interested in. I tell you. The man who put me away had more compassion. He'd have made ten of you. He . . .'

'Where were you?' snapped Belamy.

'What?'

'When Richardson was killed. Where were you?'

'I don't know.'

'Try harder.'

'At work – on the building site – or at home. One or the other.'

'Do better than that. I want times and witnesses.'

'Oh, no.' The man shook his head. He saw a uniformed constable approaching. 'That's not how it works . . . and you know it. You're making the accusation. You prove it.'

'And don't think I can't.' Belamy threw both caution and common sense to the winds. If he had an excuse, it was a poor one; that he was fed up with blind alleys. Dammit, every damn arse-bandit in town seemed to be able to laugh at the coppers, and the hell he was going to stand by and let *that* happen. He snarled, 'Smart boy, you'd better get this straight. I want answers, and *good* answers. You're not the Persil-white innocent you make yourself out to be. Richardson was murdered and by one of his kind. *Your* kind. And I'm getting ideas. Very fixed ideas. That you know a bloody sight more about that murder than you . . .'

The man wound down the car window and called, 'Constable! Constable Clarke!'

'What the . . .' Belamy closed his mouth and, fuming, waited.

Clarke came to the side of the car, and said, 'Yes, sir.' He saw Belamy at the wheel and added, 'Oh, hello, sergeant.'

In a tight but deliberate tone the man said, 'I would like you to arrest me, constable.'

'Eh?' Clarke stared.

'On the say-so of Sergeant Belamy here.'

'I'm sorry, sir. I don't . . .'

'He's just accused me of murdering Clive Richardson.'

Clarke stared across the man and at D.S. Belamy.

'That's a damn lie,' growled Belamy, but that it wasn't *quite* a lie was there in the tone and the expression on Belamy's face. He looked at Clarke and snapped, 'On your way, constable. Crime enquiries . . . that's all.'

'Oh, no.' Clarke shook his head. 'This is my beat,

sergeant. My responsibility. I know this man. I know nothing wrong about him, but if you think he's the one who murdered . . .'

'Do I hell!' exploded Belamy. 'Look, you thick-headed wooden-top, I ask questions . . .'

'Questions?' mocked the man quietly.

'. . . I'm entitled to. I don't need *your* permission. *Your* bloody beat! Judas Christ, I was wearing pavements out while you were still at . . .'

'Yes. *My* beat.' And now Clarke's temper was going. 'I'm expected to keep trouble down. Get to know people. Give the force a good name. Then you come in, slinging your weight about. Now – a fair question and a straight answer – is this man under serious suspicion of having murdered Richardson?'

'Who the devil d'you . . .'

'*Is he?*'

'No, you stupid, bird-brained bastard. He called you over because . . .'

'Because you were "leaning". I know. I've been in the job long enough to know *that*.' Clarke opened the door of the car and said, 'Go home, sir. Put it down to C.I.D. Specifically to this member of the C.I.D. We aren't all like him, thank God.'

'Thank you, constable.'

The silence as the man climbed from the car, smiled at Clarke and walked away, was as cold and as dangerous as a hanging snow-lip. One shout and the avalanche would have started moving. Belamy had the rank, but Clarke had the *right*. They stared at each other for longer than was necessary. Neither blinking. Neither prepared to unlock his gaze from the other's.

Then, in a harsh whisper, Belamy said, 'Close the door . . . *constable*.'

Clarke gave a brief nod, closed the door of the car and was on his way, continuing his patrol, before Belamy had

31

engaged gear to move the car from the edge of the pavement.

'Wardman,' murmured Helen Flensing. 'That's what Ralph says.'

'David told me.' Alva Hoyle fluffed the pillow, then nestled it back into position behind Helen's head. The hint of Welsh lilt gave the younger woman's voice a ring of honesty and common sense. 'All this waiting and playing around. I think they enjoy themselves doing things the difficult way.'

The tiny ward, much of which was taken up with the bulk of the iron lung, was spotless. Clinically spotless. It was where Helen Flensing lived, but by no stretch of the imagination could it be called 'home', and this despite the two vases of flowers, the television set and the side-table with its books and magazines. It was a prison; as much a prison as Armley, Parkhurst or The Scrubs. It was tarted up a little. The food was as good as the staff of the hospital could make it. Nurses and doctors came and went, often for no more reason than to drop in for a short chat and a smile, and as an assurance that Helen Flensing hadn't been forgotten. But despite this, it *was* a prison, and the prisoner was serving a life sentence . . . a *real* life sentence.

Alva Hoyle was not a nurse. She wasn't even listed on the staff of the hospital. But because she had a mind like blotting paper and a memory almost incapable of forgetfulness, she held a doctorate. A Ph.D. Ask her and she'd call herself a freak; what took years for normal people to assimilate she could soak up in months, sometimes weeks. She was, therefore, a Godsend as an unpaid dogsbody at the hospital. Totally reliable, she 'helped out' wherever assistance was needed; she pushed trolleys, dished out food, helped in the pharmacy or at the reception desk. Because of what she was and who she was, she was allowed free run of the hospital, and worked her own hours to fit in with the duties of her detective husband. She was appreciated because she cheerfully took orders from anybody in need of temporary assistance.

And when she'd time – always when she'd time – she called into the tiny ward and helped kill the blind boredom which was a part of Helen Flensing's life. To say they were friends would be an understatement. They knew too much about each other; had shared too many secrets; and each was a copper's wife. Few sisters were as close as Helen Flensing and Alva Hoyle.

'It's their life.' Helen smiled as she countered the younger woman's implied criticism. 'Move and counter-move.'

'Like chess, you mean?'

'Like chess,' agreed the older woman. 'And they'd better win more often than they lose.'

'And do you think the ordinary people give a damn?' There was a touch of unaccustomed bitterness in Alva Hoyle's question.

'The decent people.'

'There's not many of *them* left either.'

'Hey, honey.' Helen sounded worried. 'Come on . . . tell.'

'What?' Alva pretended to re-arrange some of the flowers in one of the vases.

'You're uptight about something.'

'Maybe,' muttered Alva.

'Okay. Unwind. I'm going nowhere in the foreseeable future.'

Alva turned her head, looked at the older woman, and said, 'I'm worried, pet.'

'Tell.'

Alva nodded a little glumly, then walked to the chair alongside Helen's head.

'They're fools,' she said gently. Bluntly.

'Our respective husbands?' Helen smiled. 'I presume that's who you're talking about.'

'Who gives a damn about them?'

'You do. I do.'

'No, I mean the people they're supposed to – what is it? –"protect". Who cares? I mean, who really *cares*?'

'Without them, there'd be . . .'

'They're called "pigs". "Gestapo". Damn, the hooligans who call them that don't know what the Gestapo were *like*. I wish they did. I wish they could have a taste. They might appreciate.'

'Alva, it gets us all at times. We don't like . . .'

'No!' The younger woman wouldn't be silenced. 'Football crowds. Rock festivals. Even cricket matches. Don't tell me the majority are nice people. That the trouble-makers are a tiny minority. If the difference was so great there wouldn't *be* trouble. A handful of policemen – anything up to a hundred-to-one – and who *helps*? Who *helps* the copper these days when the fists are flying?'

Helen remained silent. It was a mood; a mood unique to the womenfolk of policemen. And, okay, there was some truth in what Alva was saying. People – the man-in-the-street, the man-on-the-terraces – didn't like getting involved these days. Because it wasn't just fists. Not just *fists*. Broken bottles, knives, coshes . . . anything. So, the wise thing was to hurry away from the trouble.

'Do you ever think that?' demanded Alva. 'Do you ever think that your man puts everything, up to his life, on the line for people who couldn't care less?'

'Oh, yes.' Helen nodded gently. 'We *all* think about it – at least *most* of us do – at various times. If we didn't we'd be poor wives.'

'It's hell.' Alva pressed her lips together. Tightly. She wasn't too far from tears. She shook her head and continued, 'This Wardman thing . . .'

'It's not dangerous,' soothed Helen.

'Not physically. But if it doesn't work? If he doesn't break? That's Wrongful Arrest, my pet, and David's up the

34

creek.' Alva sighed.

'With Ralph. Ralph will be standing alongside him.'

'I know that. I'm not suggesting Ralph might let him down. But God! The *damages*. And the force won't pay them.'

'It's a risk,' agreed Helen.

'A risk,' mused Alva sadly. 'For a queer nobody liked. Four lives – theirs and ours – smashed if something goes wrong. No . . . if it doesn't even *work*. If the risk doesn't come off.' She sighed. 'And they call them "pigs". Louts not fit to breathe the same air call them "pigs".'

'It's a murder enquiry,' said Helen softly. 'Whatever he was, he's dead when he should be alive.'

'That . . . from you.' Alva's lips moved into a slow smile. 'My God. And *I'm* getting my panties in a twist.'

That evening P.C. Clarke's duty started at 10 p.m. and ended at 2 a.m. It was a shift he liked. Especially he liked it in mid-summer. The streets were cool after a blazing day. With few exceptions the citizenry were polite and well-behaved. The pubs closed on time, and there were rarely punch-ups because of 'fighting beer'. All in all a nice Individual Beat. Not as boring as a village beat, but the same principle. You knew most people. You wished them 'Goodnight' in passing. Sometimes you stopped for a short chat. You were *their* copper, and they appreciated that small fact. Because they knew you and became accustomed to you, the invisible barrier of uniform disappeared and they shared small intimacies with you. Asked advice. Used you as a walking adjunct to the Citizens' Advice Bureau. When you checked lock-up property it *meant* something; you knew the people who'd left that property in your keeping; knew them, respected them and did that little extra to ensure that a friendly acquaintance wasn't robbed blind by some passing breaker.

The theory of Individual Beats, of Individual Policing,

worked – as long as the guy pounding the pavements *made* it work.

Clarke made it work, smoothly and with no problems, and the mad-bull antics of Detective Sergeant Belamy still rankled. Damn, he could have done damage. *Real* damage. A happily married man, two nice kids. Screw the police –public relationship up with a family like that, and it could take months to repair the damage. Bloody C.I.D! A thing the jacks never understood. One man – one copper – hadn't a cat in hell's chance of keeping a neat and peaceful beat without the willing co-operation of the people on that beat. No way! All this bogey-man business was a thing of the past. You were either one of them, or nothing. All this thumping 'em into submission. Chucking your weight around. It didn't work anymore. Once upon a time, maybe. But these days people knew their rights. They knew how to bite back. And, anyway, who *wanted* to be hated? Who *needed* the Big Stick? Ordinary people, see? They wanted a quiet life, as much as you did. Most of 'em. Not the 'us' and 'them' attitude of the bad old days. It didn't work. It never . . .

'All quiet, Jim?'

The beat sergeant fell into step alongside Clarke as he broke into the latter's musings.

'Nice and quiet, sarge.'

'Nice night.' The sergeant eyed the darkening sky.

'Cooler than it was on the first shift.' Clarke checked a health food shop as they strolled past. 'God, it was hot this afternoon.'

'Took the kids to the baths,' observed the sergeant.

'Keep 'em cool.'

'And out of mischief.'

'They're not bad kids.' They strolled across the street to give the NatWest Bank its first check of the night. 'Like dogs. No such thing as bad dogs, only bad owners. No such thing as bad kids, only bad parents.'

36

'They're *kids*.' The sergeant spoke with the certainty of an expert. 'If there's mischief, they'll find it. *And* they're a bobby's kids.'

'Does that make a difference?' Clarke squinted through the clear-glass peep-hole in the frosted glass. 'You wouldn't want 'em to have wings and haloes.'

'They're supposed to set an example.' The sergeant sounded a mite disappointed. 'Y'know . . . behave themselves. Not yell and scream all over the bloody street.'

'Do they?'

'No more than the rest, I reckon. It just *seems* they do.'

'You're tough on 'em, sarge.'

'Maybe.' They continued their stroll. 'But every year. This blasted mid-summer break. Six weeks. They get bored to hell.'

'It's a long time,' agreed Clarke.

'I should have been a school-teacher,' growled the sergeant. 'Jesus wept, they hardly have time to sharpen their pencils but what it's one more holiday.'

'And every weekend.'

'I should have been a school-teacher,' repeated the sergeant.

They continued their company patrol. Clarke diligently checked property as they passed. He nodded silent and cheerful greeting to the occasional pedestrian. *He* didn't yearn to be a school-teacher. He was fine. This was his choice of profession, and he liked it.

The sergeant said, 'You get on well with 'em.'

'Who?'

'People. Those who live on your patch.'

'Uhu.' Clarke paused, then added, 'Until berks from the C.I.D. come in, screwing things up.'

'Meaning?'

'Belamy. He was here this afternoon throwing his weight around.'

'Enquiries?' suggested the sergeant tentatively. 'He's still on the murder rota.'

'Enquiries be damned. It was Belamy bastardy . . . pure and simple.'

'In what way?'

Clarke told him. He didn't exaggerate. It was simply a grievance which had to be aired; a setback to what he (Clarke) was trying to achieve.

'I'll have a word,' said the sergeant when Clarke had finished.

'Nothing official, please,' said Clarke. 'I credit him with doing what he thought was right in *his* way. I don't want to make trouble.'

'No. Nothing official,' promised the sergeant. 'Just a quiet word in the right ear. That he could have undone a lot of your good work.'

'That's what it boils down to,' agreed Clarke.

The South Coast Force held itself in readiness. At least, not the *whole* force, but those in the know. Wardman could be ready for collection at a minute's notice. All it needed was a telephone call.

There is, you see, a form of freemasonry between senior police officers throughout the United Kingdom. Chief constables, assistant chief constables, chief superintendents and the like . . . but not all chief constables, assistant chief constables and chief superintendents. As in every profession there are good, bad and *very* mediocre. The bond links the good with the good; it by-passes the bad and the mediocre. But where the bond exists, nothing is impossible. Nobody will let anybody down; absolute trust and absolute reliability is taken for granted. Information is passed, not from headquarters to headquarters, but from home to home. A chief superintendent in (say) Northumbria will dial the home number of an assistant chief constable in (say) Thames Valley. A home number to a home number; a call which is not logged and will not be overheard at any switchboard. Their friendship is a first-name friendship; they are both members of this select, law-enforcement cartel. Information is exchanged. Set-ups are arranged. Things are rushed or, if necessary, things are 'held'. The law is not broken . . . it is merely made to *work*.

Hoyle was a little undecided. The beat sergeant had caught him just as he was about to call it a day, and had passed on Clarke's complaint. Quietly and without fuss.

'Just a hint, sir. It might do good, and Dick Belamy can be a bit hot sometimes.'

Which was okay as far as it went, and nothing about which to get hot around the collar. But Belamy *was* C.I.D.

'You're sure Clarke wasn't laying it on a bit?'

'Not Clarke, sir. He's a good man.'

'So is Belamy.'

'But rough. And Clarke's job is to keep that beat sweet.'

'Each man to his own way, sergeant.'

'Yes, sir.' The beat sergeant nodded mock understanding. 'I just promised to have a word, off the record. That's all.'

'I'll see what I can do.'

'Thank you, sir.'

'Where is Sergeant Belamy, by the way?'

'I wouldn't know, sir.'

'Okay. It's not important. Leave it with me.'

'Thank you, sir.'

Meanwhile Belamy was having a private domestic ball.

Jean Belamy had once been a near-beautiful woman; happy, yet tranquil; neatly dressed; quietly spoken; the dream girl of at least half a dozen would-be-suitors. Come to that Richard Belamy hadn't always been an official oaf. As a working copper-on-the-beat he'd been a shade blunt and, even in those days, he'd had some very fixed ideas, but he'd also possessed a very dry sense of humour. They were

39

married and, as far as each was concerned, it was the ultimate in happy-ever-after events.

'Ever-after' hadn't lasted twenty years!

Jean had become a little plump, although she'd retained the quiet tranquillity which was part of her nature. Retained it, because she'd forced herself to retain it. Sure she still loved her husband. Had you questioned that fact she would have been genuinely outraged. But . . . put it this way. Had she *not* been married, she would never have married. The whole thing was a con. A put-on. If she *had* to be married, okay let it be to Dick. She knew him. He didn't fool around with other women. He wasn't too demanding. He worked hard, earned a moderately good wage and, as far as he was able, he made life easy for her. She could have been a lot worse. One hell of a lot worse. But, by God, if she *wasn't* married . . .

No way. No way at all!

Dick Belamy's fault?

Well, maybe so, but maybe not. From P.C. he made D.C. and as a detective constable he grew ambitious. He pulled some neat convictions off; petty thieves, pathetic perverts, the odd tearaway or two. He learned to interview and, in learning to interview he also learned that the so-called 'tough nut' wasn't too tough, after all. Apply a little pressure – threaten to tell his missus that he was having it off with some slag on the other side of town – and he'd damn near open his own cell door. That sort of thing. They all had fear. Just fish around, find what frightened them, then start turning the screw till they coughed. A reputation, you see. A reputation for making the bastards sing. And, because of this reputation, the rank of detective sergeant.

But he'd had to pay for that reputation, and the payment had been subtle and, to him, hardly noticeable. The bluntness had become coarseness. The long hours had taken their toll; he was irritable and never truly 'off duty'. The scum with which he had fought day in, day out for years had infected him with a smattering (and sometimes more than a smattering) of their own way of thought and their own manner of speech.

'Bloody pansies.' He plunged his fork into the yolk of the egg with unnecessary savagery. 'This damn town crawls with 'em.'

Egg, bacon and fried bread, at closing up to midnight. A breakfast meal at an hour when normal men have long finished supper. C.I.D. did that to a man. You ate when you could. When you were hungry, and never mind the o'clock. The snouts and the ear-hole-whisperers had to be rooted from their knot-holes whatever the time. They came before sleep, they came before meals, they came before *anything*.

Through a mouthful of half-chewed food, he grumbled, 'Then you get a pin-brained wooden-top, with a bloody great opinion of himself, shoving his . . .'

'What's a wooden-top?' asked his wife innocently.

'Eh? A uniformed nerk. What else?'

'I'm sorry. I didn't know.'

'Bloody good job we didn't have kids.' He chewed as he spoke.

'Is it?' she said in a tiny voice.

'Fifty-fifty, they'd have been queers.'

'Why do you say that?'

'Every alternate bastard you meet. A ring-snatcher or a leb. It's bloody near fashionable.'

She was in her nightdress and dressing-gown. The usual thing. When he was working late (which was more often than not) her habit was to bathe, get into her night clothes, then sit and read until he came home. It had always seemed the wifely thing to do. However late – unless he was working all night – she waited up for him. Had a meal ready. Listened to his grumbles and tried to make him unwind. It was one of *her* contributions to their married life.

She watched him as he pushed food into his mouth. This

41

man of hers. This man she'd married and had once loved. Whom she still loved. She hadn't wanted promotion. She hadn't even wanted C.I.D. She'd wanted, and still wanted, *him* . . . as he'd once been. These days he talked a language she hardly understood. More than that, he talked *at* her rather than *to* her. Just the two of them. The doctor, then the specialist, had quietly assured them. That's all there'd ever be. Just the two of them. 'Tough luck. We still have each other.' That's what he'd said and, once they were in the privacy of the car, he'd kissed her and nothing else had mattered. Not 'Bloody good job we didn't have kids.' That was now. The other had been then. The same man, but a changed man.

A great wave of sadness flooded over her.

In little more than a whisper, she said, 'I – er – I think I'll leave you, dear.'

'Aye.' He nodded. 'I'll be up later.'

'No. Not just to go to bed.' An unhappy smile touched her lips. 'I mean *leave* you.'

'What the hell?' He turned in his chair and glared.

'Not a divorce. Nothing like that.'

'Have you gone round the bend. What the bloody hell . . .'

'Not even a separation. Just a few weeks – a few months – without each other.'

'Eh?' And now he was floundering. Beneath the hard shell was the man she'd married; crying to get out, but imprisoned within what he'd forced himself to become. He said, 'What have I . . . I mean, there isn't another . . .'

'No other man,' she smiled.

'In that case, what the hell . . .'

Had the telephone bell not rung at that moment they might have talked it out. She was certainly willing, and her decision had knocked the stuffing from him for the moment. He might have listened. He might even have understood, or at least tried to understand. He loved her – make no

42

mistake about that, he still loved her – but he'd forgotten how to *show* that love. He might have remembered. Changed a little. Just enough for her to *know* that the 'other man' was still there. Still as crazy about her as ever. And had she known *that*, had he been able to convince her of *that* . . .

But the telephone bell rang.

The beat sergeant met Constable Clarke as the latter was going off duty. The sergeant's duty didn't end until 6 a.m. whereas, because Individual Policing meant starting and finishing at their home and being 'on tap' twenty-four hours a day, the beat sergeant visited Clarke's patch twice within a comparatively short space of time. It was, in fact, a couple of minutes after 2 a.m. when Clarke strolled along the street towards the house where he lodged.

'Conscientious,' smiled the sergeant as he moved into step alongside the constable. 'I've known men stand at the door for fifteen minutes before knocking-off time.'

'It's a good patch,' said Clarke solemnly.

'Good lodgings?' It was something to say.

'Home-from-home. That . . . and Liz, of course.'

'Liz?'

'Mrs Beverley's daughter. We get on fine with each other.'

'Aha,' teased the sergeant. 'The – er – the "future Mrs Clarke"?'

'It's not impossible. I suppose . . .' Clarke hesitated, then ended, 'Some people think we're unofficially engaged.'

'And are you?'

'I suppose so,' grinned Clarke.

'It's what you need as a copper, Jim.' The sergeant's tone was paternal. 'A good wife. An understanding wife.' They'd reached the gate of Clarke's lodgings. 'By the way, not much sleep tonight, I'm afraid.'

Clarke waited, questioningly.

43

The sergeant said, 'They've got a bloke for Richardson's murder. You're on for escort duty. Flensing's office at six o'clock.'

'Where from?'

'Down south. They're getting things laid on.'

'I think I'll doze in the chair,' decided Clarke. 'It's hardly worth getting undressed.'

'Civvies.'

'Of course.'

The sergeant held out a hand and said, 'I'll book you going off duty, then you can get your head down.'

Flensing and Hoyle saw no sleep that night. In the privacy of Flensing's office they sat, or paced, as the mood took them, but above all they worried. Hoyle showed his worry more than Flensing; smoked more cigarettes than Flensing; drank more cups of instant coffee than Flensing. But that was merely the nature of the man. Flensing hid his worry behind a façade of a slightly drawling voice and a mildly sardonic turn of phrase. But the worry was still there.

Hoyle eyed the slim folder on the desk; the summary of everything – every fact, every tiny piece of evidence – available in the hunt for the murderer of Clive Richardson.

He shook his head sadly, and said, 'Talk about bricks without straw.'

'My dear David, Belamy is our straw.'

'I hope so,' sighed Hoyle.

'With half what's in here,' Flensing tapped the file with a forefinger, 'Belamy could convince the archangel Gabriel that he'd played the wrong tune.'

'He'd have a damn good try,' agreed Hoyle reluctantly.

'Just don't get in his way,' warned Flensing. 'Whatever happens, let him have his head. We're not talking about interviewing. We're talking about *frightening*.'

'He'll enjoy himself,' said Hoyle heavily.

'Of course he will.' Flensing smiled.

'It's not the right way.'

'It's not "the book" way, but we've known that from the start.'

'It's ridiculous.' Hoyle lighted a cigarette before continuing. 'A detective chief superintendent, a detective chief inspector, and we risk everything on a detective sergeant we both know is no damn good.'

'Ah, but he *is*.'

'If you seriously think . . .'

'Not as a detective sergeant, but in certain given circumstances. *These* circumstances.'

'A man's conscience,' muttered Hoyle. 'A man's sense of guilt.'

'A murderer,' Flensing reminded him.

'I'm sorry.' Hoyle moved his shoulders in a half-shrug. 'I feel pity for Wardman.'

'Don't,' said Flensing gently. 'Pity for nobody, David. Or, if you *must* have pity, pity for the victim. For Richardson.'

'Nevertheless . . .'

'Wardman placed himself in this position. Nobody forced him. In effect, he made the choice.'

'He'll have all hell kicked out of him,' muttered Hoyle.

'No doubt, but, with luck, we'll be able to close the file and mark it "Detected".'

'I sit there and watch it happen? Hear it happen?'

'It's an order, David. In writing if that will help.'

'I'll be a good little chief inspector.' There was a sad bitterness in Hoyle's tone. 'I'll obey orders.'

Flensing waved a hand.

'Go on, David. Use my bathroom. There's an electric razor. We must look neat and tidy for the briefing.'

Indeed, they all looked neat and tidy and, all except the motor patrol sergeant, looked as if they'd had little or no sleep. Flensing, Hoyle, Belamy, Clarke and, of course, the

45

motor patrol sergeant. They sat in chairs around Flensing's desk and were briefed.

'It's a long drive,' said Flensing. 'Chief Inspector Hoyle will spell you at the wheel, sergeant.'

The motor patrol sergeant nodded his understanding.

'No more than four hours at a time, and when you get there stretch your legs for a couple of hours before the return journey. There'll be a meal waiting for you, but eat at least once on the way there and on the way back. The car's topped up. It will be topped up before you set off north again. But if you need re-fuelling, Mr Hoyle will pay the bill. The same when you stop to eat. Make your choice, Mr Hoyle will pay. That way there'll be only one reimbursement.'

He turned his attention to Clarke. 'You have your handcuffs with you, constable?'

'Yes, sir.'

'Good. Wardman's right-handed. Link his right wrist to your left, and do it before he leaves the cell. He sits between you and Sergeant Belamy in the back of the car. And that's as far as you go. Listen, watch, but keep your mouth shut. Your job starts and ends with getting Wardman here and into an interview room. You *might* be called as witness. If so, only to back up Sergeant Belamy and Chief Inspector Hoyle. Understood?'

'Yes, sir.'

Flensing pushed the folder towards Belamy, and turned his attention to the detective sergeant.

'Yours, sergeant,' he said.

Belamy reached forward and picked up the folder.

Flensing continued, 'Read it and re-read it on the way south. Read it and memorise it. It's all we have on Wardman . . . and it's not *quite* enough.' He moved a hand in a tiny gesture. 'Enough to arrest him on suspicion. Enough to question him. Perhaps enough to charge him with the murder of Richardson, but at my guess not enough

to be sure a jury brings in the verdict we want. It's *him*.'
Flensing paused to allow the last two words to make their
proper impact. 'Wardman is the man we're after . . .
without a shadow of doubt. On my instructions, he's been
left to sweat things out in a police cell. No questioning.
Nothing. Softening him up. He obviously doesn't know how
much *we* know. He'll be worried. He's being *allowed* to
worry. The oldest trick in the whole bag, but it always
works.'

Belamy cleared his throat, then asked, 'In the car, sir. Do
I interview him?'

'You give him hell, sergeant.' Flensing met Belamy's eyes
as he answered the question. The eyes said more than the
words. 'We need a confession. We need a statement. We
need him ready to *make* that statement when he arrives
here.'

'A free hand, sir?' Belamy glanced at Clarke as he asked
the question.

'Short of physical violence, sergeant.' Flensing gave a
quick smile, then drawled, 'I hear you have a reputation.'

'I can interview, sir,' growled Belamy. 'Especially nancy
boys.'

'First and foremost, he's a murderer.' Hoyle made the
observation, as if to concentrate Belamy's mind on priorities.

'He'll cough,' promised Belamy. Then, to Flensing, 'A
free hand, sir. No interference . . . from anybody.'

'Other than if absolutely necessary, nobody speaks to
him except you, sergeant. I estimate the journey north
should take seven hours. He's yours for seven hours,
sergeant.'

'Thank you, sir.' Belamy grinned. It was not a nice grin.
He said, 'Have the statement forms ready in an interview
room, sir.'

'I will, sergeant. Indeed, I will.'

THREE

Henry Bryant Wardman. Unmarried. Mid-forties. Plump, rather than thick-set. Clean shaven and balding fast. Short-necked and podgy-fingered.

He sat in the police cell and worried. He knew they were on their way south to collect him, but didn't know when they'd arrive. Any time now. Then the journey north. A long journey, and a very dangerous journey. It was going to be the worst journey of his life. That much he knew . . . and it worried him.

Three of the men from Lessford strolled along the promenade. The sky was still cloudless, but the breeze from the south cooled things a little and brought the tang of the Channel to their nostrils.

'Nice,' said the motor patrol sergeant. He sniffed the air appreciatively. 'Like being on your holidays.'

The waves spent themselves on the shingle, hissing and moving the tiny pebbles in the undertow.

'No sand,' observed Clarke. 'I like sand.'

'Paddling,' suggested the motor patrol sergeant with a grin. 'Give your feet hell walking over that stuff.'

Hoyle remained silent. He walked a little apart from the other two. Not because of rank – nothing like that – but because he was vaguely unhappy. Flensing? Sure, Flensing would stand alongside him if things went wrong. Flensing wouldn't duck when and if rockets started flying. But

48

Flensing didn't know Belamy. Didn't really *know* him. Take the brakes off Belamy, and he'd crack steel girders. Sure. But he wouldn't do it gently. No subtlety. No real skill. He'd pile-drive a confession, think he'd done something great, and end up by screwing everything to hell and beyond. That was Hoyle's worry. That Flensing had given Belamy an open cheque and Belamy might go mad.

The object of Hoyle's thoughts was half a mile behind them, on a promenade bench. Belamy had read and re-read the file all through the drive south. He was re-reading it again. Carefully. Virtually word at a time. This was his big case. *His* case. Flensing had handed it to him on a plate, and as far as he (Belamy) was concerned, he'd never have a finer launching pad. Detective sergeant be damned. This one could make him detective inspector. Detective chief inspector. Maybe even detective superintendent.

Wardman, and the smashing of Wardman, was the key to his future. Then listen to Jean, eh? All that crap about leaving him. Christ, you don't leave a man with a future. Not if he's a good husband. Not if he doesn't fool around with other women. She'd change her mind. Smartish. Bloody women! They didn't know when they were well off. Didn't know. Couldn't recognise a bowl of cherries when it was there in front of them. Sure he worked. Over the years he'd worked his arse off. And what for? For a *name*. For a *reputation*. Well, it was his for the grabbing now, and no way was he going to pull back his hand. A good job, a good salary, a good pension. Bigger. Fatter. All he had to do was break this perverted gink Wardman.

God help Wardman!

The other three had turned and were approaching the bench. Hoyle said something to them, quickened his stride a little, then sat down alongside Belamy.

'Ready, sergeant?' Hoyle tried to sound and look pleasant.

'He's mine,' said Belamy.

'Not quite enough.' Hoyle nodded at the closed file.

'Plenty.'

'I mean to stand him in court.'

'With his own statement, he'll go down,' growled Belamy.

'Maybe.'

'Look.' Belamy thrust his chin out a little. 'As I understand it, the boss gave *me* this case.'

'True.' Hoyle nodded.

'I don't want Clarke shoving his oar in.'

'Why should he?'

'He's that type. Too bloody soft for real policing.'

'It's possible,' murmured Hoyle gently.

'So, as a favour, keep him quiet.'

'I'll have a word with him.' Hoyle glanced at the folder again. 'The smudged prints,' he remarked.

'Wardman's no expert.' Belamy touched the file with a finger. 'Seven smudged prints. Total of ten matching characteristics.'

'Pushing things.'

'I'll push.'

'I don't have to remind you.' Hoyle sighed. 'A minimum of fourteen matching characteristics on *one* print, otherwise it's inadmissible as evidence.'

'Wardman doesn't know that,' insisted Belamy. 'I'll handle Wardman.'

The motor patrol sergeant and Clarke strolled past the bench. They neither looked nor paused. They continued their stroll along the promenade.

Hoyle bent his head, clasped his fingers between his knees and stared at the ground. He spoke in a soft tone of near-defeat.

'My money says you won't break him, sergeant. Short of physical violence – and *I'll* not tolerate that – all he has to do is keep saying "No". We take him north. You talk your head off. But unless *he* starts talking, we might as well give

50

him his train fare back here before we set off.'

'He'll talk.' There wasn't a hint of doubt in Belamy's words. 'He has previous convictions. *They'll* start him talking, and once he starts I'll make damn sure he doesn't stop.'

'I wish you luck.' Hoyle raised his head, unclasped his fingers and stood up. 'Let's go. We've a long drive ahead of us.'

Clarke sat in the offside corner of the rear seat of the Cortina. He eased the bracelet of the handcuffs on his left wrist and spoke to Wardman.

'Comfortable?'

Wardman nodded, but said nothing.

In the nearside corner of the rear seat Belamy closed the file for the last time and slipped it into the door pouch. He remained silent and stone-faced. He had all the time in the world. Already he'd summed up the man Wardman. Soft. A typical pansy. A seven- to eight-hour drive ahead, including stops. He'd skin him alive. He'd have the perverted bastard weeping blood, long before the end of the journey.

The motor patrol sergeant was at the wheel. Hoyle had said, 'Get us north of London, sergeant. I'll take over when we hit the motorway.' A wise decision. The sergeant had slept the previous night, and in addition he could handle a car with police-trained expertise. It wasn't quite rush-hour time, but the traffic was building up. The Blackwell Tunnel was like a target at which the local drivers aimed rather than drove their vehicles; get in the wrong lane and it was hell's own job easing a way back into the correct lane.

Hoyle grumbled. 'The bloody road numbers. Don't they use them down here?'

'Shoreditch,' said the motor patrol sergeant quietly. 'Get there, we're on the A1. We pick up the M1 at Hendon.'

An eight-wheeler thundered past, missing them by less

51

than three inches.

Hoyle said, 'Christ! They all have a death wish.'

Belamy ignored the traffic. He turned slightly in his seat; angling himself into a position where he was more easily able to talk directly to Wardman. From an inside pocket he took a notebook and ballpoint. He glanced at his wristwatch and noted the time at the head of a new page.

Almost conversationally, he said, 'Not the first time.'

The prisoner didn't seem to hear him.

'I'm talking to you, Wardman.'

'Oh!' Wardman seemed to pull himself from a brown study and raised his head.

'Not the first time,' repeated Belamy.

'What?'

'Homosexual fun and games. Thumping people.'

'Oh . . . that.'

'Yes, *that*.'

'I don't have to say anything,' muttered Wardman.

'Who imparted that piece of priceless information?'

'I was told. I was cautioned.'

'Bully for you.' Belamy chuckled. 'You're going to sit there, like tripe, all the way north. Is that it?'

'I don't have to say anything,' repeated Wardman.

'We don't *need* you to say anything,' lied Belamy. 'We have you bang to rights, sonny. You wouldn't be taking this ride, otherwise.'

'In that case, why ask questions?'

'Questions?' Belamy looked surprised. 'Who's asking questions? Stating facts, lad. That's all I'm doing. Stating facts. Giving advice.'

'Advice?'

'Forget it, sonny.' Belamy turned his head a little and stared out at the traffic.

'What sort of advice?' insisted Wardman.

'You don't want to know.'

'Yes, I want to know.'

52

'Just help yourself,' said Belamy airily.

'I'm sorry, I . . .'

'Nobody else is going to help you, Wardman.' Belamy turned his head. 'Get that. Get it fixed. *You*. Nobody else gives a damn. The court can send you to Outer Siberia. Who the hell cares?'

'The – the court?'

'The Crown Court. The old boy in the wig and ermine. That's your destination. Hasn't anybody told you?'

'They – they suggested I killed Clive Richardson.'

'Sure.' Belamy nodded.

'*But I didn't.*'

'Crap.'

Helen Flensing asked, 'Do you know this Sergeant Belamy?'

'I've met him.' Alva Hoyle nodded. 'Last year's Police Dance. His wife's a nice enough woman.'

'What about him?'

Alva pulled a face and said, 'Not my type.'

The door to the tiny ward was locked. They were breaking one of the minor rules of the hospital. Two-woman cheese and sherry parties were *not* part of the hospital routine. A minor infringement and one the authorities would, no doubt, have accepted without too much fuss; after all, one of the women couldn't attend a similar normal function and the other woman was held in high esteem. Nevertheless, against the rules. It was one of the score or more things which cemented their friendship; an almost schoolgirlish disregard of unimportant do's and don'ts. Like midnight feasts in the dorm. Like wearing a skirt just the inch higher than authority demanded. Trivialities which were more than trivialities.

Helen closed her lips around a tiny cube of cheddar, pulled it off the cherry-stick and chewed. She sipped wine before she spoke.

'David couldn't have done it.' It was part-question, part-statement.

'No.' Alva chewed, then swallowed. She grinned and added, 'Too much of a gentleman.'

'He's with them.'

'Ah, yes. But only to make sure Belamy doesn't kick Wardman's head in.'

'That would be funny.' Helen's chuckle was part-giggle.

'Not for Wardman.'

'Would he?'

'What?'

'Belamy. Is he capable of something like that?'

'He's a slob.' Alva topped up the glasses. 'Pity we've only one bottle. We could get stoned and pull faces at the matron.'

They were on the A1 at Highgate, travelling north. The traffic had thinned a little, but the motor patrol sergeant knew London.

'We're ahead of the rush, but when it comes it'll come like a jet from a hosepipe, all the way to Watford. Bumper-to-bumper, every lane, and going like the clappers.'

'Can we beat it?' asked Hoyle.

The sergeant nodded at the windscreen and said, 'I'll keep ahead of it . . . with luck.'

In the rear seat, Belamy had settled down to a prolonged interrogation.

'You keep feeding me a load of crap.'

'No. That's not . . .'

'You were in Lessford.'

'I admit that. I'm not . . .'

'You knew Richardson.'

'Well, all right. But that doesn't mean . . .'

'You visited him.'

'He was a friend. Why shouldn't . . .'

'He was as big a queer as you are.'

'I'm not – I'm not . . .'

'And now he's pushing daisies.'

Wardman nodded miserably.

'For Christ's sake, come clean,' hammered Belamy. 'Last person to see him alive. We have statements, sonny. Witnesses. Last person to see him alive . . . first person to see him dead.'

'No!'

'You're a damn liar and we can prove it.'

'You can't prove I killed him,' whispered Wardman.

'Don't bet on it, sonny. Take my tip . . . don't bet on it.'

They passed between East Finchley and Golders Green; that stretch of the A1 called Lyttleton Road.

The motor patrol sergeant grunted, 'Hendon coming up.'

Hoyle tried to divide his attention between the traffic and what was happening in the rear of the car. The tiredness was hitting him; it came and went like long, rolling waves; for about an hour or so he'd feel normal and able to concentrate, then the loss of a night's sleep, plus the weariness of the drive south, would make his eyelids droop and bring on yawns of fatigue. It required a distinct effort of will to push the tiredness aside, light a cigarette and concentrate on what was happening.

Belamy was saying, 'What do *you* say you were doing in Lessford?'

'I'm a rep.'

'A commercial traveller?'

'If you like.'

'Hawking what?'

'Sweets. Confectionery.'

'On commission?'

'A salary plus commission. My sales book's in with my property.'

'So, it will show where you called.'

'Er – not at Lessford. Bordfield.'

'Now, there's a thing,' mocked Belamy. 'You hawk at

55

Bordfield but stay at Lessford. Why?'

'I prefer Lessford.'

'Richardson's place?'

'I sometimes stay there.'

'Only "sometimes"?'

'I visit. I don't always stay overnight.' Then, with a spat of annoyance, 'It's no different and no worse than staying with some fancy woman.'

'Except that Richardson was your fancy *man* . . .'

'Look. Can't you . . .'

'. . . and you left him dead, with his head caved in.'

'That's not true.' But Belamy's technique seemed to be having some effect. The denial lacked its previous outrage. Without it being a mere token denial, it no longer had bite. It lacked real conviction.

Clarke was linked to Wardman by the handcuffs. He could feel the slight but slowly increasing fidgeting of Wardman's hand. The unease of his prisoner. The lack of certainty. Like the pause of a dynamited structure after the explosion but before it crumbles. He felt compassion for the man. Even pity.

With his free hand he fished in his jacket pocket and said, 'A cigarette, Wardman. It might . . .'

'*Shut up!*' Belamy almost screamed the words. Then in a quieter, but harder, tone, 'No cigarettes. Nothing! Keep out of it, Clarke. Keep well out of it. The bastard's a murderer. No sweets and candy for this sod. No cigarettes. Just you . . .'

'Cool it.' Hoyle spoke from the front passenger seat. Then to Clarke, 'Just sit there, constable. Sit there, and stay quiet.'

'Yes, sir.'

Poor Jean Belamy. All she wanted was to feel *needed*. Loved a little. Not too much . . . she'd have been satisfied, even happy, to have known she was loved just a little. Needed.

56

But to have *known*. Not just having to guess. Having to take it for granted. To be *told* . . . just occasionally.

She dabbed her eyes with a handkerchief as she fought to come to terms with herself. With her life. With her marriage.

Of course she wasn't going to leave him. Of *course* she wasn't. Not for a week. Not for a day. Women like her didn't 'leave' their husbands. Stupid women – immature and silly women – played at those games. Whatever else she was, she wasn't *that*. He'd changed. *She'd* changed, she supposed. Everybody changed, but nobody *thought* they changed. Other people, but never them. That was the mystery, and at the same time the tragedy.

Once upon a time . . .

Oh yes, once upon a time he'd been a nice man. 'Nice'. Meaning a little thoughtful. Easier to live with. More of a gentleman and less of a policeman. Not smarmy. Not smooth. Sometimes not even too polite. But – y'know – *nice*.

On the other hand . . .

Two sides to every coin. A right and a wrong in every argument. Maybe *she* was at fault. Maybe she didn't try hard enough to understand his side of things. The hours he worked. The terrible people he was expected to bring to justice. The shocking things he was forced to witness.

Nor was she the perfect, glossy magazine-type wife. She was no cook. She tried – God knows, she tried – but it never came out quite right. Sometimes it was a disaster. She couldn't sew. Again she tried, but never with real success. Everthing *looked* home-made. The same with knitting. The same with just about everything. So what was left? Companionship? But she couldn't enthuse about football, cricket bored her and she didn't understand snooker – his main television viewing. Reading? He didn't read books. He hadn't *time* to read books. He was far too tired, and nothing in print could equal his own real life. Music? He was completely stone deaf as far as music was concerned.

Pop groups he loathed, and that she could understand. But the other stuff. The *real* music. Symphonies. Operas. Concertos. 'Turn that bloody row off.' His immediate and instant reaction.

And yet he was a good man. A good husband. He drank little, smoked little, didn't gamble and was in no way unfaithful. A good man and *her* man.

The damn job. That was the reason. The *real* reason. Not her, not him, not the fact that they couldn't have children. The job. A de-humanising job. A job for morons, and if a man wasn't a moron it turned him into one. Ruthless. Demanding. Refusing normal social life. Refusing such things as uninterrupted sleep or proper meal times. Twenty-four hours a day for thirty years ... then a pension. My God! A pension. Take a man, smash him, tear the guts and soul from him, then reward him with a pension for the few years he had left. Few ex-coppers drew their pension for long. They were old men before their time. Soured and unsmiling. Fit only for the knacker's yard. Hated by those they'd tamed. Mistrusted by those they'd protected. 'He used to be a policeman.' The number of times she'd heard that remark. Like a condemnation. As if he'd been in prison; committed some terrible crime; was somehow beyond the fringe of decent society. 'He used to be a policeman.'

Jean Belamy's gentle misery left her. She'd found a whipping boy. The job. Not her, not her husband. Policing, and how it changed a man.

'You are,' said Belamy harshly, 'a fornicating idiot.'

'I don't know what you're talking about.'

Belamy grabbed the file from the door pouch. He flicked it open and said, 'Previous offences, sonny. Oxford, Darlington, Leeds, Bristol. Tough-guy antics. G.B.H. Throwing your weight about generally. You've been inside for it. What's murder to a creep like you?'

'I haven't murdered anybody.'

'Crap.'

'You have a very limited vocabulary.'

The M1 stretched ahead of them. Mile after weary mile of it. Four hours, five hours, maybe more counting stops. One hell of a journey. A long way, but was it long enough? Had Belamy enough time? Could he nudge, push, con or frighten this man Wardman into a confession?

Wardman seemed to fluctuate. He'd reach almost breaking point then, when he was about to topple, he'd pull back. But maybe – just *maybe* – he was getting a shade nearer the edge each time. Clarke could feel the tiny spasms of trembling as if nerve ends, beyond Wardman's control, were quivering at some invisible strain being placed upon them. Belamy, too, could feel them and it pleased him. It meant there *was* a breaking point – there *was* a weakness – and given time and technique he could reach it. He turned the pages of the file and stabbed one of the glossy black-and-white photographs with a finger.

'That's how the cleaning woman found him, and *that's* how you left him, sonny.'

'No.' But it was a half-hearted denial. No outrage. No indignation. Not the explosive denial of an innocent man.

'You were seen going in.'

'I've said. I visited him, that's all.'

'What time?'

'Midnight. Thereabouts.'

'That's not what the statements say.'

'They're wrong.'

'Hell's teeth, don't you think we checked and double-checked?'

'All right. *I'm* wrong.' Wardman tried to move the hand which was connected to Clarke. 'Midnight. *About* midnight. I can't give the exact time. Who can?'

'The witnesses,' suggested Belamy.

'I – I wasn't there long. And he was alive when I left.'

'You intended spending the night there.'

Wardman nodded.

'You've as good as admitted you *did* spend the night there.'

'When? When did I say that?' The gabbled question-cum-denial held panic.

'You were seen leaving early next morning.'

'No!'

'You were *seen*, sonny.'

'It's a mistake. It has to be. I – I didn't stay. He – he didn't want me to stay. Didn't invite me. I – I don't stay where I'm not wanted.'

In the front of the car the motor patrol sergeant murmured, 'We've beaten the rush. Snooze till the next service area, then you can take over for a spell.'

'Thanks.' Hoyle settled himself comfortably in the seat and closed his eyes.

Clarke, too, would have liked to have slept; to have relaxed in the corner of the rear seat and cat-napped a little. But it was impossible. Each time Wardman moved, the handcuff gave a tiny jerk to his wrist. The handcuff and, of course, Belamy.

Belamy, the epitome of that American expression for a detective, 'a bull'. On and on and on; mixing truths with lies and half-truths; pile-driving away, like a punch-drunk boxer slamming a canvas bag. How many innocent men had this loathsome man put away? How many times had some unfortunate cried, 'Enough!' and signed a confession to some crime he hadn't committed. For the sake of peace. As the only means of silencing that ugly, grating voice with its never-ending accusations. That stupid 'sonny' with which he bespattered his talk. As if Wardman wasn't a grown man. As if he was a half-wit.

Clarke glanced at the man he was handcuffed to.

Middle-aged and running to fat. A worried look. Worry

60

bordering upon panic. But with previous convictions for violence and under suspicion for murder who wouldn't be worried? Who wouldn't panic? Not a pleasant man . . . obviously. But that didn't make him a murderer. That didn't give Belamy the right to harass him this way. What the hell it said in that file wouldn't stand up in court. That was patently obvious, otherwise Belamy wouldn't be hammering as hard as he was. It *couldn't* stand up in court. Just that Belamy was out to make a name for himself. 'Give him hell, sergeant'. That's what Flensing had said. An order. 'Give him hell.'

But for God's sake don't smash him into an admission of something he hadn't done. Flensing didn't mean *that*. Just – y'know – make *sure*. Eliminate the doubts. Don't 'fix' the poor bastard. Chief superintendents didn't give *those* orders, ever!

'You're in the house.' Belamy drove forward remorselessly:
'I called,' muttered Wardman.
'More than "called".'
'I was in the district. Richardson was my friend. I called to see him.'
'To spend the night.'
'He didn't invite me, so I didn't stay.'
'Just "Hello" and "Goodbye",' mocked Belamy.
'Not much more than that.'
'Why?'
'What?'
'Buddies. Bedmates. Why didn't he ask you to stay?'
Wardman shook his head and shrugged.
'An argument?'
'No. Why should we argue. We were friends.'
'You're an argumentative type, sonny.'
'I don't know where . . .'
'Your previous cons, boy. You are a *very* argumentative type.'

61

'We didn't argue,' mumbled Wardman.

'You just called?'

Wardman nodded.

'Because you were friends?'

Again Wardman nodded.

'At *midnight*?'

'I – er . . .' Wardman nodded a third time. 'About then.'

'A hell of a time to go calling?'

'I'd been busy.'

'Oh, sure.' Belamy's lip curled. 'Very few sweet and tobacconist shops close before midnight.'

'It's not just a matter of getting orders.'

'No?'

'There's paperwork.'

'Where did you do the paperwork?'

'In the . . .' Wardman closed his mouth suddenly.

'In where?' teased Belamy.

'In a boozer. At Bordfield. I often do it that way.'

'In a boozer?'

'Uhu.'

'Which boozer?'

'Eh?'

'The boozer? The name of the pub?'

'I – er – I dunno.' Wardman shrugged. 'Just a pub. Handy.'

'In Bordfield?'

'Yes . . . in Bordfield.'

'But you don't know its name?'

'I didn't look.' Then after a tiny pause. 'It had a car park.'

'That,' sneered Belamy, 'cuts the number down considerably.'

Wardman let the remark pass.

'So.' Belamy eased his shoulders. 'A pub at Bordfield. Till when?'

'Closing time.'

'Then to Lessford and Richardson's place?'

Wardman nodded.

'Richardson kept late hours, did he?'

'Yes. Er – usually.'

'You didn't have to get him out of bed?'

'No.'

'He was dressed?'

'Well . . . more or less.'

'Meaning?'

'Pyjamas. Dressing-gown.'

'Is that a fact?' The question had dangerous overtones.

'He was – he was ready for bed, I think.'

'Alone?'

'Yes.'

'Just the two of you?'

'Yes.'

'Doing what?'

'Y'know, talking.'

'Just . . . talking?'

'That's all.'

'How many times did you use the bathroom?' asked Belamy suddenly.

'I – er . . .' Wardman frowned concentration. 'I didn't. I didn't use the bathroom. I – er – I had no need.'

'You lying bastard.' Belamy's voice became a soft, snarling roar of derision. 'He was mother-naked. His dressing-gown was still in the wardrobe. His pyjamas – newly washed and ironed – under the pillow and un-touched. Who the hell answers the door at midnight without a stitch on? *And* your dabs were all over the shower curtain. All over the tiles of the shower cubicle. Stop feeding me crap, sonny. What the hell d'you think we are? Mugs? Why d'you think you're here? D'you think we closed our eyes and shoved a pin into a list of names? You, sonny. *You*! You're the hound we're after. You are 'it'. You slaughtered the miserable slob. Good riddance . . .'

'No. I have a key . . .'

'. . . but you're the louse responsible.'

'. . . I let myself in.'

'Come again?' sneered Belamy.

'I – I have a key to his place,' breathed Wardman. 'Y'know, a key. I – I let myself in. Then – then later. I asked if I could use the shower. That's all. I swear . . . that's all.'

'A shower?'

'I was grubby. I'd been on the road all day.' The explanation was being gabbled. 'I needed a clean-up. I asked him, and he said it was all right.'

'Then you *talked*,' mocked Belamy.

'Yes.' Wardman nodded desperately. 'We – we talked. That's all. Then I left.'

Belamy stared his contempt into the face of the sweating Wardman. For almost a minute the detective sergeant remained silent. A spitting, derisive silence.

Then he said, 'When will you learn, Wardman? You're a liar. You're *still* a liar.'

'I didn't hear all that.'

'No, sir.'

Gilliant, be it clearly understood, was a good chief constable. Some said too good. He'd been chief for a long time; since the amalgamation of Bordfield City, Lessford City and a socking great area of the connecting and surrounding County Constabulary in 1976. That had been in the days when 'big is beautiful' had ruled the corridors of power in the Home Office, and *that* particular theory had broken the back of more than one chief constable who'd figured himself an Atlas type. Not so Gilliant. Gilliant had carried the massive responsibility with comparative ease, mainly because he chose his senior officers with care and, having chosen them, delegated responsibility without shoving his nose into every pie. Nevertheless, he knew what was happening throughout the force — *demanded* to know what was happening — and because a murder enquiry seemed to be grinding to a halt, he'd visited Lessford D.H.Q., and for the past hour or so had been closeted with Flensing, listening to the detective chief superintendent's explanation of what was happening.

And now he smiled and said, 'I didn't hear all that.'

'No, sir.' Flensing returned the smile.

'Belamy?' Gilliant raised a questioning eyebrow.

'Chosen with great care, and at the right time.'

Gilliant nodded slowly.

'Hoyle I'd trust with my life,' added Flensing.

'It may almost boil down to that.'

'I thought you should know . . . off the record.'

'I'm obliged.' Gilliant settled back in his chair. It was a deliberate movement; it signified that as from that moment they were talking as friends and not as fellow-officers. He said, 'Ralph, I feel age creeping on. Not physical age — I'm as fit as I've ever been — but just "age". The job. The way it's turned back on us.'

'All of us,' agreed Flensing.

Gilliant said, 'Somebody from Outer Space dropped in to see us. Took things at their face value . . . they could be excused for thinking *we* were the criminals.'

'Some of us are.' Flensing's tone was sombre. 'That "Countryman" thing. Get a mob like the Met able to stonewall a genuine enquiry into corruption, and by senior and experienced officers, there's something very sour somewhere. Just occasionally you get glimpses of it.'

'Just occasionally,' agreed Gilliant.

'About a year ago,' continued Flensing. 'We'd nicked one of their villains. A couple of detectives came north to collect. A sergeant and a constable.' He sighed. 'I swear. Their clothes — including overcoats — tailor-made and top-class quality. Damn it, some of them are so used to it they don't seem to realise it stands out a mile. *I* couldn't afford

65

to dress that way.'

'It's a backlash,' opined Gilliant. 'Call a force – any force – bad loud enough and long enough and a percentage of them will say, "Okay, let's be what they *say* we are and make the most of it.". There's a deal of truth in it, you know, Ralph. A community gets the police it deserves.'

'Men like Belamy,' grunted Flensing.

'They get through the net,' sighed Gilliant.

'And then,' added Flensing wryly, 'you use them . . . but very dangerously.'

'What a magnificent mental picture,' sneered Belamy. 'Both of you. You and Richardson. Starkers. Sitting there *talking* to each other.'

Just for a moment Wardman seemed to find courage enough to fight back.

He said, 'Sergeant, you seem to have a very unhealthy obsession with the naked male body. Homosexuality intrigues you. I wonder why?'

Belamy's eyes rounded and glared. His nostrils quivered.

Wardman turned to Clarke and murmured, 'Wouldn't you agree, constable?'

Before Clarke could speak, Belamy exploded. 'Hold it! Hold it right there, you perverted bastard. A warning. I have a very short fuse as far as creeps like you are concerned. Don't risk anything, sonny. Don't even *think* of being funny. This is the last car you're going to ride in for a hell of a long time. Bear that in mind whenever you feel like being jokey. *You are going behind granite*. That I promise you. For murder. For murdering your twisted little friend, Richardson. For caving his skull in . . . after your peculiar little chit-chat. So don't start . . .'

Hoyle had jerked awake at Belamy's roar of outrage. The sergeant was steering the car off the motorway and up the gentle slope to the service area.

Hoyle said, 'We stretch our legs here. Ten minutes or so. If anybody wants a pee now's the time.'

66

FOUR

It was one of those summers; one of those sizzling, sweating, when-the-hell-is-it-going-to-cool-off summers. On the meteorological maps high pressure areas were rolling in from the north west like a string of red-hot pearls. The farmers were griping, the gardeners weren't happy, the water boards were calculating how many days it would be before hosepipes were banned, but the holiday-makers were having a whale of a time. The beaches at the candy-floss resorts were carpeted with human flesh being barbecued. The hotels and guest-houses were bursting at the seams. Half the population of the United Kingdom seemed to be swigging booze, guzzling ice cream, buying cheapjack junk, pouring money into the cash-boxes of fun-fair proprietors or splashing around in sewage-contaminated waves.

The other half were sitting in their cars, bumper-to-bumper, wondering when the engine was going to explode.

'Do we stay on the motorway?' asked the motor patrol sergeant.

'We have the fast lane,' observed Hoyle.

'The overtaking lane,' corrected the sergeant.

'At least *one* lane.'

'There's roadworks ahead,' warned the sergeant. 'I noticed them coming down.'

'So? What advice?'

'Six and two threes,' sighed the sergeant. 'The other roads might be just as jammed.' He paused, then added, 'If

Wardman tries anything on the motorway he's a dead duck.'

'Tries anything?' Hoyle looked puzzled.

'He hasn't a lot to lose.'

'He's handcuffed to Clarke . . . and stays that way.'

'Uhu.' The sergeant moved his hands in resignation. 'The motorway then. And remember . . .' he gave a slow grin.

'I know.' Hoyle nodded. 'Drive as if every other driver on the road is a blind drunk raving maniac.'

'The only safe way,' agreed the motor patrol sergeant.

The toilets were full. Men were waiting patiently for an empty stall. The place stank of urine and antiseptic. Clarke and Wardman stood in the queue side by side, and when they talked it was side-of-the-mouth conversation. Little more than a whispered communication.

Clarke said, 'Keep your right hand in your jacket pocket, I'll keep my left hand in mine. Nobody will notice the handcuffs. Find two stalls alongside each other.'

'As if you cared.'

'We aren't all called Belamy.'

'You're all coppers . . . same thing.'

'Don't be a bloody fool.'

Each seemed to have a strange anger and disgust for the other. Strange, because in the car Clarke had tried to make Wardman as comfortable as possible, despite the handcuffs, and Wardman had given the impression of appreciating this. But now there was almost open antagonism.

'Don't equate me with that bastard sitting alongside you,' whispered Clarke.

'*You* sit alongside me.'

'You know what I mean.'

'You're all dog-dirt. Some of you don't *think* you are, that's all.'

'Over there.' Clarke jerked savagely with his right wrist

68

and led the way towards two vacant stalls alongside each other.

There was black humour in two men, each with one hand in his jacket pocket, unzipping, urinating, then zipping up their trousers. A few of the strangers gave puzzled glances, but few guessed the truth.

'Why don't you chalk broad arrows on my coat?' hissed Wardman.

'Finished?'

'If you have.'

'Right, let's get out of here.'

A man in a hurry tried to barge between them, but Clarke closed shoulders with Wardman and the man apologised before swerving to one side.

'Fun and games,' growled Wardman.

The remark seemed to trigger off convulsive fury in Clarke. He elbowed and shouldered his prisoner round two corners away from the crowd. There was a short, blind-alley behind the toilets and the side wall of the café entrance. Clarke pulled his left hand from its pocket, spun Wardman, jerked the prisoner's arm high behind his back and pushed him, face-forward, against one of the walls. Then, when he spoke, Clarke's voice was harsh with anger, little more than a whisper and with his mouth no more than six inches from Wardman's ear.

'Listen, scum. What you are – whatever *else* you are – you're something of a tearaway. You've been inside for it, remember? Violence. You go for violence in a big way. But don't get wrong ideas. I *don't* like violence, but by Christ I can *be* violent if necessary. So, don't act the smart-arse with me. Don't count yourself bigger or better than I am. Don't stand me alongside men like Belamy. Yourself . . . sure. You're two of a kind. But not *me*. We have a long journey ahead of us. You'll need all the friends you can grab. Don't go out of your way to make enemies . . . understand?'

'You're my friend?' sneered Wardman.

'I'm nothing. I'm the post you're chained to. No more than that. Concentrate on Belamy. Concentrate on Hoyle. You have more than your hands full.' The flash of fury seemed to cool as suddenly as it had come. Clarke released Wardman's bent arm and returned his hand into the jacket pocket. In a calmer voice, he said, 'Right. Let's get back to the car.'

'Who's Wardman?' asked Helen Flensing. 'What's he like?'

'A hard man, so I'm told.' Flensing's mind seemed miles away. He sat alongside his wife and his shoulders sagged a little, as if the present burden was much heavier than its usual weight. He gave a deep breath which ended in a long sigh, and added, 'I've never met him. I don't know him personally.'

'You're taking a lot for granted,' mused Helen.

'More than usual,' he agreed heavily. Then, 'Gilliant knows.'

'Oh!'

'He called in. I thought it wise to tell him. Not "officially", of course.'

'Why? Why tell him?' She was genuinely puzzled.

He compressed his lips for a moment, then said, 'If things go wrong – badly wrong – we might need a cover-up.'

'And he'll help?'

'He might. He'll do all he can.'

She gazed at him in silence for a moment, then said, 'I never thought I'd hear you say that.'

'What?'

'"Cover-up". It's not *you*. It's not the way you work.'

'We're talking about murder,' he muttered.

'Policing,' she corrected.

He rubbed his left eye with the fingertips of his left hand. God, he was tired. Not just because he hadn't slept for two days. Other reasons. Worry. Decisions. Decisions he'd made, but hadn't wanted to make. Decisions that went with the job . . . if all else failed.

'Policing,' he said gently, 'means putting a man in a dock with enough evidence to secure a conviction.'

'The *right* man,' she insisted.

'The man we *think* is the right man.'

'And are you sure?' she asked.

He nodded.

'So what's the use of a jury?'

'The jury is the long-stop,' he sighed. 'So is the judge. The same with the law of evidence. We're human. We can make mistakes. We try not to, but . . . sometimes.'

'And this time?'

'As sure as we'll ever be.'

'But with room for a mistake,' she teased.

'Helen, darling, don't make it worse.' She was woman enough, wife enough and wise enough to know she'd said the wrong thing. She caught the hint of a groan in his words, noted (not for the first time) the predominance of grey in his thinning hair. He said, 'It's a gamble. If Belamy can't break through we have to let a murderer walk free, or arrest with insufficient evidence.'

'I'm sorry,' she said sadly.

'It's part of the job.' He smiled. 'The job gets harder by the month, by the day almost, but it has to be done . . . somehow.'

Hoyle drove a little more slowly than the motor patrol sergeant. The last thing he wanted was a shunt, and the traffic was dense enough to demand total concentration. Cars hauling caravans swung into the centre lane, tried to overtake speeding lorries but couldn't, and the overtaking lane became filled with speeding cars with only an occasional gap into which he could slide the Cortina. Motorway driving! Just one fool and it became assembly-line carnage.

71

The motor patrol sergeant relaxed in the front passenger seat and listened to the battle being fought behind him. He was interested. Very interested. Belamy was of the C.I.D. The elite . . . or so they considered themselves. Well, give him motor cars every time. Wardman was scum. Okay, Wardman was scum, but so was Belamy. The only weapon he knew was 'the frighteners', and maybe it was working, but on the other hand maybe it wasn't. He (the motor patrol sergeant) wouldn't have broken. He'd have told Belamy to get knotted . . . then closed his mouth.

Wardman didn't seem to have the sense to close his mouth.

He said, 'We *talked*.' The tone was impatient with having to repeat the same answer over and over again. 'People *do* talk, sergeant. They hold intelligent conversations. It's a bit old-fashioned, I know, but some people . . .'

'What did you talk about?' interrupted Belamy.

'I forget.'

'Be wise, sonny. Start remembering.'

'Books, I suppose. Films. Television. The usual topics.'

'What sort of books?'

'Books we'd read.'

'Which films?'

'Films we'd seen.'

'Which television programmes?'

'Those we'd watched.'

'Right.' Belamy's voice moved down a semitone. 'Now, let's stop dodging round corners and be specific. I want names of films, books, programmes – what the hell you talked about – and I want to know what *you* thought of 'em and what *he* thought of 'em.'

'Is that important?'

'It's important . . . because I *say* it's important.'

'It won't turn me into a murderer.'

'You're that, already. It *might* turn you into a bigger liar than you are.'

72

'I think we talked about recent television plays.'

'Real culture vulture stuff.'

'The adverts.'

'The *what*?'

'I sell for a living. What induces people to buy interests me.'

Belamy grunted.

'Books?' Wardman frowned. 'I think we agreed that *The Noel Coward Diaries* was very enjoyable.'

'Another homo,' growled Belamy.

'A damn good book.' The motor patrol sergeant spoke from the front seat.

'Who asked?' demanded Belamy.

'Just in case you haven't read it,' replied the sergeant.

'Just drive the bloody car,' snapped Belamy.

'It's *being* driven.'

'You know damn well what I mean.'

'Hey, Belamy.' The motor patrol sergeant half-turned in his seat. 'You're neither God nor the Son of God. You might think you are, but no way. Talk to Wardman any way you please, just don't think you can talk to *anybody* that way.'

'You're not very popular, Sergeant Belamy,' murmured Wardman.

Belamy moved his head in a slow, nodding motion. A movement which suggested the reaching of a decision, and the ending of what *he* might have called 'patience'. He grabbed Wardman's free hand and, as he spoke, he flicked each of the fingers in turn.

'Arches. Loops. Whorls. Double-loops.' His tone was softer than before, but more savage. He almost threw the hand away, as he continued, 'Ridges and islands. Bifurcations and terminations. We all have 'em, Wardman. Everywhere. All over our body and everybody different. Touch something, with any part of you, and it's like leaving a signature. *Your* signature. Unique. Fingerprints . . . get it?'

'All right.' Wardman gave the impression of being bored. 'I have fingerprints. I left them at the house. I *was* at the house. I called to see Clive Richardson. So what?'

'Called to see him?'

'Uhu.'

'Or called to *kill* him?'

'Not to kill him . . . to *see* him.'

'To have a shower?'

'It seemed a good idea. He agreed.'

'Therefore your dabs on the shower-curtain?'

'Of course.' Wardman nodded.

Belamy paused, then said, '*In blood?*'

'What the hell are you talking about?' But there was the shadow of a tremor in the question.

'What's Richardson's blood group, sonny?' asked Belamy.

'I don't know.'

'*I* do. Clive Richardson, blood group AB.'

'I can't see what . . .'

'The trap under the shower, sonny. The boffins emptied it. Lots of water. Diluted blood. Group AB.'

Wardman's lips tightened and he remained silent.

Belamy continued, 'The dabs on the shower-curtain. Fingerprints. *Your* fingerprints. *Bloody* fingerprints. Blood group AB. Now . . . start lying your way out of that little lot.'

'You're bluffing,' breathed Wardman.

'No way.' Belamy tapped the folder holding the file. 'That's what it says here. That's what we can prove. Twenty years inside . . . that I promise.'

'I didn't kill him.' It was like a plea from a drowning man; a final anguished sigh in a sea beyond sight of land.

Belamy was worried. A tiny, nagging worry which lodged at the back of his mind and refused to be brushed aside. Belamy was a copper and, moreover, a moderately

74

efficient copper. That at least. That he had been coarsened by the job was resultant upon his own character, but in no way detracted from the basic fact that he was a professional. Ergo, the worry.

Flensing had given specific orders. 'Give him hell, sergeant. We need a confession. We need a statement.'

Why?

The right time, the right dabs, the right blood group. This boyo didn't need pushing. He didn't need cracking. He was already a horrible heap of rubble in the dock of any Crown Court in the country. Belamy knew it. Flensing *must* have known it.

So, why the job? Why the statement?

Okay, he'd do it. He'd been told to do it, he was paid to do it and, if the truth be told, he rather enjoyed doing it. Making the foul bastards squirm. Rubbing their noses in their own dirt. And, fine, a statement would pin him down but good, but it wasn't *needed*.

The worry wasn't big enough to stop him. It wasn't even big enough to slow him down. But it was *there*.

Clarke, too, worried. Fingerprints, and bloody fingerprints at that. The right blood group in the showertrap. My Christ, this Wardman was in trouble. Over the eyes in trouble. As for the statement Belamy was trying to drag out of him . . . that was just policing. Driving the last nail in an already firmly lidded coffin.

And Wardman, moreover, was a nerk. God Almighty, he'd seen the inside of prison, which meant he'd undergone all this red-necked treatment before. A violent man stays violent when he reaches a nick. He might not stay *physically* violent, but his nature doesn't change. At some time in the past – and more than once – Wardman had been subjected to hard interrogation. He knew the score. He knew the name of the game. So, why in hell's name was he coughing? Why wasn't he just sitting there, letting Belamy spout off till his voice ran out?

The whole damn thing was wrong. Screwy. Worrying.

Belamy gave himself a rest. He lighted a cigarette, smoked it for a few moments, then started on a new and, on the face of things, a more moderate tack.

'All right, sonny. You didn't kill him. You arrived at midnight, showered, then sat talking to each other in the nude, then you dressed and left. Okay?'

Wardman nodded.

'That's all crap, of course.' Belamy left the door wide enough not to have it slammed in his face, then continued, 'But just to make you happy we'll pretend it *isn't* crap. What next?'

'I'm sorry, I don't . . .'

'You've left Richardson alive and kicking. Contrary to expectations, he hasn't asked you to stay for the night. What did you do when you left?'

'Drove back to Bordfield.'

'And?'

'Booked in at a hotel.'

'A hotel?'

'A guest house, really.'

'I don't give a damn – guest house, hotel – which guest house?'

'I – er – I didn't notice its name.'

'Oh, for Christ's sake!'

'It was late . . .'

'You bet your sweet life it was late.'

'. . . and I stopped at the first place I saw a light.'

'But you don't know it's name?'

'I'm a rep . . .'

'I know. A commercial traveller.'

'. . . and I move around a lot. A different town every night, almost.'

'So, who pays the bill?'

'The firm.'

'So, you *get* a bill?'

'Of course. They wouldn't . . .'

'Presumably the name of the hotel, the guest house – whichever dump you sleep in – is there on the bill?'

'Naturally.'

'Great.' Belamy nodded. 'Bed and breakfast?'

Wardman nodded.

'So, all we have to do is check your property and there it is. The bill, with the name of the guest house printed on top . . . and *that* part of this fairy story checks out.'

'It's – it's not in my property,' muttered Wardman.

'Surprise, surprise.'

'I – er – submit them each week. With the week's orders.'

'But it's still around. Somewhere.'

'You're not going to believe this,' groaned Wardman.

'I'm not surprised. I haven't believed a bloody thing so far.'

'They've lost it. Misplaced it.'

'The bill?'

'I don't know where it is. I submitted it along with all the other papers, but it's been lost.'

'If it ever existed.'

'It existed.'

'Wardman,' sighed Belamy, 'you should have your voice trained.'

'Eh?'

'The funnies you come out with – the way you tell 'em – all you need is an exit song. There isn't a variety club in the United Kingdom wouldn't pay you to top the bill. A good song, a few tap-steps . . . you're made.'

'You don't believe me?'

'That's a damn-fool question to ask.'

'All right.' Wardman hesitated, moistened his lips, then said, 'I spent the night in the car.'

'No hotel?'

'No . . . I'm sorry.'

'No guest house?'

'No.' Wardman sighed.

'No bill?'

Wardman shook his head.

'Sonny.' Belamy put mock-pleading into his tone. 'Would you *know* the truth if it sat up and begged for peanuts? Would you *recognise* it?'

'Look.' Wardman seemed to reach a decision. 'I'm scared, sergeant. That's the truth. I'm shit-scared. Wouldn't *you* be in my position?'

'I wouldn't know.' Belamy's voice was dead-pan. 'I've never murdered anybody.'

North of Luton and Dunstable the traffic seemed to ease a little. The impression was the motorists had reached their homes and were resting before changing to return to the road for the evening. Later they might be visiting pubs or friends and the weight might increase, but for the moment Hoyle was prepared to accept the ease of continued concentration without questioning its cause.

'Next service area?' asked the motor patrol sergeant.

'The one after that,' replied Hoyle.

'Newport Pagnell.'

'Is it?' Hoyle held back a yawn. 'We'll have a break there, and something to eat.'

The patrol sergeant grunted agreement.

Hoyle had been listening to the verbal exchange going on behind his back. Reluctantly – *very* reluctantly – he found himself feeling some degree of admiration for Belamy's technique. Bull-in-a-china-shop stuff? Sure. But the gaps were there, too. The silences. The spaces in which a guilty man's conscience worked like the very devil.

A man had two ears, but only one mouth. Good detectives remembered that simple fact. Listen twice as much as you talk . . . you're around to *hear* things. The trick was to create things worth hearing.

Meanwhile . . .

Alva Hoyle wandered around the rooms of their home, using her hands in an attempt to slow down her mind. Emptying and polishing ash-trays. Straightening the magazines and newspapers in their rack. Re-arranging the scatter cushions on the sofa and chairs. Anything to stop the growing anxiety about her husband's future.

Poor David. He worked so very hard. He'd made detective chief inspector on sheer graft and, if this foolishness went wrong, it would have all been in vain. She knew her husband. Understood him better than most wives know their man. A plodder . . . certainly a plodder. But he never *stopped* plodding. That's what made him different – better – than his fellows. That's what made him utterly trustworthy, and *that* was why Ralph Flensing had chosen him for this silly caper.

If it went wrong David wouldn't complain. Ralph would back him – for sure Ralph would back him – but David was the man-on-the-spot and, because he was the man-on-the-spot, he wouldn't dodge the rockets. He wouldn't take cover behind the 'obeying orders' excuse.

Of course, things might *not* go wrong. Belamy might do what everybody hoped he would do. The odds were slightly in that favour. A car – a steel box on wheels – and four police officers. The psychology was great. Trapped and surrounded by enemies. It had to have *some* effect. Not the old interview room set-up. Something he'd seen before. Something he knew about. But to be enclosed in a speeding motor car . . . Well, maybe.

Look on the bright side, Alva girl. Ralph thinks it can be done, and Ralph is nobody's fool.

'What did you do with the weapon?'

Belamy broke the long silence with a very direct

79

question.

'What?' Wardman seemed to jerk out of thoughtful misery.

'Whatever you bashed his brains in with. We haven't found it.'

'I didn't kill him.' The tone was lost. A tone of defeat, without timbre.

'Let's assume you *did* kill him . . .'

'I didn't.'

'. . . or didn't *mean* to. What did you hit him with?'

'Won't you believe me?' pleaded Wardman.

'Tell us where the weapon is.'

'I didn't *use* a weapon.'

'Look at this, sonny.' Belamy opened the folder and found the photographs. He chose a close-up of the battered skull. He held it in front of Wardman's face. 'That's not done with fists. The proverbial "blunt instrument". Where is it?'

'I didn't use one.'

'Crap, where is it?'

'I don't know.'

'Or you won't tell?'

Wardman's mouth twisted into a bitter smile as he said, 'It doesn't matter too much of a damn, does it?'

Belamy returned the photograph to its place, closed the file and spoke with what, for him, was a reasonable and reasoning manner.

'Wardman, correct me if I'm wrong. The yarn . . . as I understand it. You hawk sweets. You're at Bordfield. You know Richardson who lives at Lessford. Instead of booking in at some hotel for the night you drove to Lessford, to Richardson's place, at about midnight. You have a key. You let yourself in. Richardson wasn't expecting you, but he didn't object. He didn't tell you to shove off. Not immediately. You had a shower. Then both of you – Richardson and you – sat there, starkers, and talked about

80

books and such. Then – reason unknown – Richardson *did* tell you to shove off. You dressed, left and spent the night in your car. That it, so far?'

'That's it,' mumbled Wardman.

'Why did he change his mind?'

'What?'

'He didn't tell you to blow when you first arrived. Let you have a shower, in fact. Why did he shoo you out later?'

'We . . .' Wardman moved his shoulders. 'Y'know.'

'No. I don't know.'

'A bit of an argument.'

'About books?' There was mockery in the question.

'No. Other things.'

'What other things?'

'I – I can't remember. He – y'know – had a bit of a temper.'

'Two of you,' observed Belamy.

'Eh?'

'You've been inside for it, sonny. That temper of yours.'

'Oh!'

'Two of 'em with bad tempers,' mused Belamy. 'An argument and one of 'em ends up dead. Your ticket's well and truly marked, sonny.'

'*I* didn't kill him.'

'Somebody else there, was there?'

'No.'

'You suggesting he battered *himself* to death?'

'Don't be silly. Of course not.'

'So . . . *who?*'

'I don't know. But not me.'

'You're the only pebble left on the beach, sonny. It *has* to be you.'

'Not me.' It was a whispered denial. No real denial at all.

'Don't be bloody stupid. Of course it was you.'

'Oh, God!' Clarke felt the steel encircling his wrist pull his hand away from his body, as Wardman dropped his

81

head into his hands, rested his elbows on his knees and wept quietly. 'Oh, my God. Help me. Help me to make them understand.'

The way of an interview. If you have the right man, he breaks. It may take hours, it may even take days, but given guilt, the truth can be dragged from him. The word 'No' – the expression 'Not me' – can be repeated only so many times. Eventually, it becomes meaningless and some other word or expression must be substituted.

The hard boys would not agree. They would argue that only mugs cough. That only canaries sing. To sit there, dumb, is all that is needed, but that, too, is impossible.

All a good interviewer needs is a reaction to his questioning. Not even answers. Insults will do. The verbal bridge is built; words are being exchanged; anger and contempt on the part of the interviewee suffices. The cough will come later.

Hoyle drove north with an easier mind. Belamy had done what both he and Flensing had prayed Belamy would do. The murderer would crack. Nothing surer. Nothing more certain.

The motor patrol sergeant turned his head and spoke to the weeping Wardman.

'Easy, old son. Nobody's going to touch you.'

Belamy smiled, but remained silent.

The motor patrol sergeant wriggled in his safety harness, fished out a newly-laundered handkerchief, shook it out and held it over one shoulder.

'Here.'

Wardman raised his head, then with his free hand took the handkerchief.

'Thanks.'

He wiped his eyes and blew his nose.

The mind of the murderer was in a turmoil. Agony,

indecision and terror jostled for first place, and the mix was such that his skull seemed to throb – to expand and contract with each heartbeat – until concentration was almost impossible.

Belamy wanted a cough. Belamy wouldn't be satisfied with anything less. A complete written admission of guilt. Signed and witnessed. No messing. No argument. No excuse. The cold-blooded killing of Clive Richardson.

And it hadn't *been* like that.

Self-preservation, see? As simple as that. A smashed life or an ended life. Richardson had been a bastard. A hateful bastard. If ever a man had deserved to die it had been Richardson.

But . . .

Belamy wasn't going to be satisfied with anything less than a complete cough.

Hoyle growled, 'Not bloody likely.'

'Eh?' The motor patrol sergeant jerked himself from his reverie.

'They're damn near queuing up to get in.' The Newport Pagnell service area was in view and, as Hoyle remarked, the impression was that every alternate vehicle was turning off the motorway and into the café area. 'The next junction, I think.'

'Junction fifteen.'

'We'll turn off. Find somewhere quiet and have a real meal.'

It had been hot for too many days. Hot, sticky and stifling. The whole country had been stewing in its own sweat for far too long and the thunderheads gathered out over the North Atlantic and gathered speed as they moved south-east. They hit Northern Ireland, clipped the south-west of Scotland and raced south over Cumbria. Cleveland, North Yorkshire and Lancashire took the cloudbursts, then South Yorkshire, Humberside, Lincolnshire and Cheshire. It came suddenly, like the closing of heavy curtains. The sun was blotted out and in its place lightning flashed and thunder rumbled.

The Cortina raced north and into it. At first rain-spots as big as 10p pieces, then the downpour, stair-rod straight and bouncing from the bonnet and the road surface to a height of almost six inches. The 'fast' position of the windscreen wipers could hardly keep pace with the rain and the spray thrown up by heavy vehicles. It was suddenly dark enough to need headlights at dip, while about and along the skyline forked and sheet lightning played a fugue with the constant rumble and crash of thunder.

Hoyle eased his foot off the accelerator and slid in behind a lorry using the middle lane. He gradually slowed the speed of the Cortina in order to distance the bonnet from the mist thrown up by the rear wheels of the lorry.

'Ease back a little farther,' advised the motor patrol sergeant.

Hoyle obeyed and, as he did so, a low-slung sports car overtook on the right.

The motor patrol sergeant virtually foresaw the sequence of events before they happened.

'Left trafficator,' he snapped. He glanced over his left shoulder and added, 'Into the slow lane, and keep the trafficator going.'

The sports car was going too fast for the weather conditions. Its wheels 'planed' on the water-covered surface and lost adhesion with the road.

'Onto the hard shoulder,' ordered the motor patrol sergeant.

The sports car slewed out of control, nudged the steel barrier and was thrown back towards the lorry which had been in front of the Cortina.

'Brake . . . slowly. To a stop.'

The lorry swerved slightly in an abortive attempt at avoiding an accident. The sports car hit the lorry, spun, then rolled and turned as its radiator smashed into the barrier and, suddenly, the scream of tormented rubber mixed with the crash of thunder, and the harsher smash of crumpling metal accompanied the continual shimmer of lightning.

'Brake!' The patrol sergeant shouted the word, and Hoyle brought the Cortina to a halt.

The lorry swung to its left, crossed the slow lane and the hard shoulder, mounted the banking, straightened, teetered then came to rest at a crazy angle on the slope of the banking. The rear of the lorry was less than ten yards from the nose of the Cortina. To their right they could hear the bump and crash of a multiple pile-up even above the noise of the storm.

Hoyle breathed, 'Jesus wept!'

'Belamy, inspector, lend a hand.' The motor patrol sergeant was already half-way out of the car. 'Clarke. Stay here with the prisoner.'

It had suddenly stopped being an escort job – a crime enquiry – and turned into a major road accident. The motor patrol sergeant's territory. The motor patrol sergeant was in charge. Hoyle didn't hesitate. After a moment's hesitation, Belamy accepted the changed situation.

'Up front.' The motor patrol sergeant waved a hand. 'The sports car driver. See how he is.' Hoyle and Belamy weaved a way between the puzzle of vehicles, while the motor patrol sergeant hurried to the cab of the lorry. The driver of the lorry looked dazed – blood was running down his face where his forehead had collided with the driving mirror – but he was conscious and swearing blue murder about mad bastards who shouldn't be allowed behind a wheel.

'Police!' The motor patrol sergeant interrupted the flow of bad language. 'You on citizen band?'

'What the flaming hell was the barmy . . . ?'

'*Are you on citizen band radio?*' shouted the motor patrol sergeant.

'Who the hell . . . ?'

'I'm a police sergeant – never mind the clobber, that's what I am – now, answer the question.'

'Yeah.' The driver nodded a dazed affirmative. 'I'm on C.B.'

'Check that it's still working. If it is, call for immediate assistance. Get things moving . . . don't just sit there feeling sorry for yourself.'

'What the . . . ?'

'*Do it!*' exploded the motor patrol sergeant. 'Police. Ambulance. Have a fire tender ready in case some damn fool decides to light a cigarette.'

The advice was necessary. The storm was at its peak and the motorway was flooded to almost two inches of water. God only knew why, but the sports car hadn't sparked itself off into a ball of fire, nevertheless the tank had been ruptured and the green-yellow streaks of escaping petrol floated on the surface of the rain-water; it had already spread well away from the wreckage and was flowing under and around the dozens of stationary vehicles.

As he hurried towards Hoyle and Belamy the motor patrol sergeant kept up a steady shout of, 'Switch off your engines. For God's sake don't strike a match. Switch off your engines everybody. The road's running in petrol. No matches. No cigarettes, for Christ's sake.'

A handful of drivers with that extra bit of gumption than most of their fellows left their vehicles, braved the weather and moved among the mix-up passing on the warning.

Fifteen minutes later the local force had taken over. A uniformed inspector was with Hoyle, and the two of them were leaning into the wreckage of the sports car.

'I think he's still alive,' said Hoyle. 'Unconscious and trapped, but alive. We haven't moved him. I've a suspicion his spine might have taken a beating.'

The uniformed inspector grunted agreement, straightened and turned towards the police cars parked on the central reservation. The cars were surrounded by uniformed men already kitted out for the weather. He pointed as he shouted his orders.

'You, get that ambulance here in a hurry. Then the fire service, with foam, before the place becomes an inferno. You and you, find the tail-back and stop any lunatic who thinks he can weave a way through. You and you, up front. Start unknitting it, but push 'em until you're well clear of the petrol. And names and addresses of possible witnesses. We'll get the statements later.' Then, in a quieter voice, and to Hoyle, 'The stupid sods never learn. They'll drive slightly better for about a week. After that, they all think they're back on Brands Hatch.'

At junction fifteen Hoyle swung the Cortina from the motorway and onto the A508. He drove slowly until they saw an inviting public house which displayed a sign advertising *meals now being served.*

'Try here.' He turned into the car park alongside the pub. 'Something hot. Somewhere to dry ourselves out, perhaps.'

Their schedule had gone to hell. It was almost two hours since the sports car had skidded and created a monumental motorway snarl-up.

FIVE

'They're going to be two hours late. At least two hours late.' Flensing (for Flensing) was agitated. The voice was still a soft drawl and, other than a slight tightening of the lips, the expression remained, as always, on the verge of sardonic. Nevertheless, he *was* worried. 'Murphy's Law . . . if a thing *can* go wrong it *will*.'

He gazed from the window of the tiny ward and watched the renewed sunshine draw hazy steam from the soaked surface of the car park. The storm had passed Lessford, and already the early evening sun was building up the heat. Twice in the same day he'd visited his wife. Not *so* unusual but, as she knew, one reason for the second visit was a means of seeking solace. It was a measure of their closeness. Other men went home, found the nearest bar and tippled a double-whisky or opened their heart to a colleague. With Flensing it was his wife. He didn't need help. He didn't need advice. All he needed was the company of somebody he could trust and somebody who understood him. It was nice to know. Nice to know that even though she was imprisoned she was *needed*. She was a vital part of this man she worshipped.

She smiled and said, 'If I know David, he won't allow the delay to change things.'

'Uhu.' He nodded agreement at the window before he turned. 'But y'see, dear, it's the *interruption* that's important. God knows how far Belamy was from a break, but from what David could say on the phone Belamy had his hands full dealing with the accident. He'll have lost the thread. He'll have to pick it up again.'

'And can't he?'

'I don't know.' Flensing sighed gently. 'He's not the world's best interrogator, and in effect he's back at square one. The man he's trying to break will have had a second wind. Assuming he was toppling – maybe he was, maybe he wasn't, I don't know – but assuming he *was*, he'll be upright again by this time.'

'You make him sound like a factory chimney.'

'To demolish.' Flensing's voice sounded tired and, perhaps, touched with bitterness and/or defeat. 'Why do these writers always assume the copper enjoys himself. The thriller writers. The television and film scriptwriters. The man in charge of the hunt always enjoys himself. He doesn't . . . hardly ever.'

'They don't handle real life,' she soothed.

'They should.' He flopped into the chair alongside her head. He stretched out a hand and linked fingers with hers, gently. 'We hunt men, not animals. Our own kind.'

'Not *quite* your own kind.'

'I could kill,' he said softly. 'Those who put you where you are. I could kill them . . . personally. I'd be wrong, but I'd feel justified. Why should I enjoy hunting a stranger who's killed another stranger? At a guess, *he* felt justified.'

She squeezed his fingers, momentarily, then said, 'You think too much.'

'As I've said.' A smile brushed past his lips. 'We demolish. Destroy. It might be nice to construct for a change.'

The pub was a typical country hostel. South of Northampton, tucked away along a road between villages. Plenty of oak, a lot of horse brasses, a hunting horn, an ancient muzzle-loader, a few prints, a handful of faded photographs, but no dirt. The wood- and brasswork shone. The chairs and benches were unstained and comfortable. The food was plain but plentiful.

Hoyle had taken the landlord to one side, explained who they were, where they'd been and where they were going. A side-room – a 'snug' – had been set aside for them. Thereafter ham and eggs, apple-pie and cheese and lashings of hot sweet tea. A three-bar electric fire helped to dry their clothes.

The door of the room was closed and Wardman sat on a wall-bench between Belamy and the motor patrol sergeant. The handcuffs had been removed in order to allow him to eat with more ease.

'I think it's stopping.' Hoyle cocked his head to one side and stared through the window. 'I think the clouds are breaking.'

'It'll be close on midnight before we reach base,' observed the motor patrol sergeant. He was in his shirt sleeves. His jacket was hanging on the back of a chair to one side of the electric fire. 'These jaunts. They're a hell of a lot farther than they look on a road map.'

'Always,' agreed Hoyle. Then generally, 'Anybody want a drink before we leave? I'm having whisky.'

The motor patrol sergeant asked for a shandy, Belamy asked for whisky, Clarke asked for a half beer.

'You?' Hoyle directed the question at Wardman.

'Nothing, thank you.' Then after a pause, 'I'd like to use the toilet.'

Clarke sighed and pulled the handcuffs from his pocket.

'The – er – bowels. Not the bladder.'

'Oh!'

Hoyle said, 'Go with him, constable. No need for the bracelets.'

The two men left the room, Clarke gathering a bunch of material at the wrist of Wardman's jacket, holding it firmly in a clenched fist. The standard manner of keeping a nonviolent prisoner under control. In the toilets, Clarke checked the W.C., released his hold on the sleeve of Wardman's jacket, then stood back by the stalls to wait.

Wardman closed and bolted the door, glanced up and saw what he'd hoped was there; a gap between the partition and the ceiling. The gap was quite wide enough. Without hesitation, he put a foot on the toilet, grasped the top of the partition and hoisted himself up, keeping well to the wall. He wriggled his way as fast as he could across the adjoining W.C. cubicle then saw the window above the wash-basin, and the wash-basin was hidden from view in an alcove as deep as the W.C. partitions.

He moved with cautious speed. Down, until he was squatting with feet on each side of the basin. Carefully he turned the cockspur fastener on the pebble-glassed casement window, pushed the window open and threaded a leg through the opening. Then the foot remaining on the edge of the wash-basin slipped, Clarke heard the clatter and was in time to see Wardman literally diving towards freedom.

Belamy saw the escape through the snug window. Without consciously watching, he saw the pebble-glassed casement window open outwards; the outer wall of the toilets ran at right-angles to the main building of the pub and the topography was such that, looking from the window to check the weather, it was impossible *not* to see the cement-rendered wall of the toilets. He therefore saw the escape, and for a moment didn't *realise* what he was seeing. When realisation dawned, he let out a roar of outrage.

'Jesus Christ, he's getting away!'

Belamy left his seat only a shaved second before Hoyle and the motor patrol sergeant. They bunched at the doorway of the snug, sorted themselves out, then raced out and into the still-pouring rain. Belamy was ahead, followed by the motor patrol sergeant with Hoyle making a poor third. Clarke joined them and raced after Hoyle.

Wardman ran awkwardly. He seemed to limp a little. The impression was that he might have twisted his ankle. That, plus the soggy grass along which he ran . . . he *had* to be caught.

Belamy reached him first, smashed a shoulder into the small of his back and, as Wardman sprawled, the detective sergeant turned him, dropped with his knees on Wardman's chest and swung lefts and rights at Wardman's face. Wardman twisted and covered his head with his arms, but more than one hard-clenched fist landed and, before the motor patrol sergeant could pull Belamy clear, blood from burst lips was running from Wardman's mouth.

For perhaps five seconds genuine fury sparked between Belamy and the motor patrol sergeant.

'What the thundering hell . . . ?'

'Leave him. He's caught. He's re-arrested. There's no need to smash . . .'

'Stick to your bloody motor cars. Don't shove your nose into . . .'

The motor patrol sergeant sank a fist, wrist-deep into Belamy's middle, and the detective sergeant doubled then sank to the ground.

'There's more where that came from,' panted the motor patrol sergeant. 'I'll not stand by and . . .'

'Cool off . . . both of you.' Hoyle's voice carried the authority of a chief inspector who knew his rank, and knew how to carry that rank. 'Get back inside. Clean up.' Then to Clarke, who had already closed the handcuffs around Wardman's wrists. 'Take *him* inside, too. Do whatever's necessary to his mouth. Then – all of you – your drinks are waiting. Knock them back, then let's get on our way.'

Hoyle worried. Talk about 'the best laid schemes of mice and men'! Interview him, that's what the man had said. Talk. Break him. Have him ready and eager to sign a statement admitting everything.

Oh, sure, sure.

Barring motorway pile-ups. Barring thunderstorms. Barring two blasted sergeants eager to knock hell out of each other. Barring everybody being soaked to the skin. Barring so many things.

Dammit, it wasn't going to work.

No *way*!

Alongside him, the motor patrol sergeant drove the car with a grim-faced determination which borded upon sullenness. Immediately behind his back Belamy seethed; Hoyle could almost *feel* the glare of steel-hard hatred directed at the back of his neck. Wardman was re-linked to Clarke, but now Wardman had a split mouth and a bruise was coming up on his left cheek-bone . . . and that helped things along not at all.

Hoyle took a deep breath, then fished for cigarettes. He lighted one. He offered the packet to nobody. The hell with 'em. If it happened, it happened. If it didn't . . .

God, he was tired. What the hell some of the others felt like . . .

Well, one good thing, they seemed to be running out of the weather.

Nevertheless, he worried.

They drove north towards Leicester; past the M6 interchange; out of the storm and into early evening sunshine. Their clothes dried on their backs and the inside of the Cortina felt a little like the interior of a laundry.

In a low voice Wardman said, 'I shouldn't have run.'

Nobody answered him. His swollen lip tended to make the words come out slobbery, but they were understood. They were heard, but nobody answered him.

'Panic,' he added.

Still nobody replied.

'It makes it look worse than ever, doesn't it?'

The impression was that he *wanted* to talk. That he was

anxious to say something, given the chance. Given a listener willing to hear him out.

He muttered, 'I know how it looks, but I didn't kill him.'

'Not *that* again.' Belamy's voice was heavy with disgust.

From the front seat Hoyle said, 'You tried to get away. Innocent men don't act that way.'

'If they're frightened.'

'If you're innocent, you've nothing to be frightened of.'

'Oh, yes.' Wardman's tone was acrimonious. 'So many times, inspector. Innocence and guilt don't mean a thing. You people get hold of us, we're scared. We have cause to be.'

'Not with *us*,' argued Hoyle.

'That why I had a hammering?' With his free hand Wardman touched his swelling cheek. 'I was down. Caught. But this bastard here couldn't keep his fists off me.'

'If,' said Hoyle in a flat voice, 'you have a complaint, make it. We'll note it. *I'll* note it. Here. Now. There'll be a report sent in.'

'Oh . . . big deal.'

'You miserable, misbegotten sod, *you're a murderer.*' Belamy could contain himself no longer. The blind loathing, the limitless contempt, the boundless repugnance. There was no make-believe. No shouting. No blustering. It was all there, naked and uncontrolled. His voice trembled with disgust. 'Lower than the animals, you and Richardson. The world can do without both of you. But *you* killed him. Battered him to death . . .'

'No. I didn't kill him.'

'. . . And that means you have to be taken inside. God knows how much cost. Rate-payers. Tax-payers. For filth like you . . .'

'I keep telling you . . .'

'. . . And now you have the blind bloody impudence to *complain*. You! Scum like you . . .'

'I'm not complaining,' mumbled Wardman. 'There's

two of us . . .'

'Don't you bloody-well dare.'

'Cut it out in the back there.' Hoyle stopped what was boiling up to a verbal war. In a quieter tone he said, 'Wardman, if you've anything to say to Sergeant Belamy, say it. Just say it. And sergeant, your likes and dislikes are your affair. They don't belong to this situation. Sit on 'em.'

Belamy took a deep breath, then murmured, 'Yes, sir.'

'I didn't kill him,' said Wardman wearily.

In a controlled, hard voice, Belamy said, 'You're a liar, sonny. And we can prove you're a liar.'

'They'll be late. It'll be past midnight.'

'Don't worry, pet. Ralph phoned and asked me to slip in and tell you . . . that's all.'

Helen Flensing examined the reflection of the younger woman in the angled mirror. Alva Hoyle was a truthful person, and a close and intimate friend, but there was always that room for doubt. A helpless invalid, you understand? That's enough for anybody to cope with. Keep as much bad news from her as possible.

'Nothing more?' she asked and, as she asked the question, she watched the reflection carefully.

'An accident,' said Alva. 'A motorway pile-up. They had to stop and lend a hand.'

'Nobody hurt?'

'Some stupid driver going too fast. He was . . .'

'No. I mean our people.'

'They're all right. All of them. They weren't involved. They just had to stop and help . . . that's all.'

Helen nodded, slowly. Almost convinced.

Alva strolled to the medical prisoner and turned one corner of the sheet farther from Helen's face.

'Don't *do* that.' Irritation was wrapped around the words.

'Helen, my love.' Alva raised mildly reproving eyebrows.

95

'You don't know, do you?' The elder woman seemed to be anxious for an argument. 'Nobody knows.'

'We try,' said Alva soothingly. 'But, as you say, we don't know. Like closing your eyes and pretending to be blind. But we know we can open them again and see. Therefore, we don't know.'

'No condescension, please.'

'You want a fight?' Alva grinned wickedly. 'Say the word, pet. We'll fight if that will make you feel better.' The grin broadened. 'Mind you, where *you* are I'm odds-on favourite.'

'I'm a cow,' muttered Helen.

'Sometimes,' agreed Alva. '*I'd* be a cow with that thing wrapped around me.'

'You're sure they're all right? All of them?'

'Ralph rang . . .'

'Why didn't he ring me?'

'There's a switchboard. Switchboards have operators. And operators sometimes eavesdrop.'

'Oh!'

'Satisfied?'

'I – er – I suppose so.'

'Helen, my lovely.' The hint of a Welsh lilt added brittleness to the criticism. 'Your man isn't there. My man *is*. If anything had happened – if *anybody* had been hurt – I wouldn't be here, playing Mut and Jeff with a bad-tempered female locked up in a stainless-steel oil drum. I'd be on my way south . . . if I had to run every inch of the way.'

Helen's mood softened. She sighed deeply, then said, 'I want this thing over and done with . . . that's all.'

'Give it time.' Alva's tone, too, moved to their normal friendly plateau of gentle banter. 'Your old man's a wily old fox, and mine runs him a close second. They're doing it "right", see? Take a step wrong – just one step – the whole thing might fall apart. I don't think it's ever been done this way before. If it has, nobody's ever said so.' She gave a quick, chuckling giggle, then added, 'But they wouldn't, would they?'

The motor patrol sergeant wanted to get home. He pushed the speed of the Cortina to a steady seventy and weaved expertly from the centre lane to the overtaking lane, then back to the centre lane. Motorway driving as it was meant to be. Swallowing the miles like a hungry man sucking in a long length of spaghetti. The road surface had dried and, to the left, the sun moved towards a multi-coloured horizon. The weight of traffic had eased; Nottingham and Sheffield were already named on the junction mile-plates; the countryside was changing. The North. Make no mistake. The 'North' *was* different from the 'South'. Harsher, but at the same time more friendly. Grubbier – oh, yes, grubbier, with more wasteland, more tips and more broken-down, once-upon-a-time factories and warehouses – but more homely. None of the 'flash' of the so-called Home Counties. None of the great lush meadows. None of the stockbroker belt homes with huge, immaculately kept lawns and weedless flower beds. Instead, sprawling farmland surrounding houses and outbuildings of grey, lichen-covered stone. The land up here had to be *worked*. It gave its produce – certainly it gave its produce – but it had to be *made* to give its produce.

Land, villages, towns and even cities which sat atop of the great coalfields. And men worked on the surface as savagely as they worked under the surface. Energy and food. And graft, of course . . . the word having its Northern meaning, and not the meaning clothed by dubious characters who haunted the shadows of the Big City.

The motor patrol sergeant's mood mellowed. The North, you see. Such a hell of a lot better, such a hell of a lot more honest than the South, but of course the motor patrol sergeant was a Northerner.

97

'What did you do with the weapon?' asked Belamy.

'I didn't kill him.'

Wardman mouthed the four-word denial, but without hope. It had become stupid. Stupid and meaningless. It had to be said, but for what impression it made it needn't have *been* said.

'Not the poker,' insisted Belamy. 'Nothing like that. From the shape of the wounds more like a pick-haft. That's what the pathologist says in his report.'

'I don't possess a pick-haft. Never have.'

'Something *like*.'

'Nor anything "like".'

'A car-jack handle?' suggested Belamy. 'You have a car.'

'I didn't kill him.'

'Something there, in the house. Something you took away when you left.'

'I didn't take anything away.'

'What did you use, sonny?'

'I didn't use anything. I didn't kill him.'

'What did you do with it?'

'For God's sake, sergeant, give it a rest.'

'When I've got there.'

'Where? Where for heaven's sake?'

'The end. The winning post. When I know everything I want to know. Not what I *need* to know, sonny – I have that already – what I *want* to know.'

'You have enough already,' grunted Wardman.

'The only true remark you've made so far.' Belamy nodded.

'You're going to fix me,' said Wardman sadly.

Belamy nodded.

'Why?'

'You killed Richardson.' Before Wardman could reply, Belamy continued, 'You say not . . . that makes *you* a fool. The fingerprints, the witnesses, the blood group. We can *place* you. You even admit to being there. Sit on a jury, sonny. Any jury on earth. Listen to what *we* have to offer, then balance it against what *you* have to offer. You haven't a cat's chance.'

'That doesn't mean . . .'

'It means,' interrupted Belamy, 'that if we can trot out the old madam about "the prisoner helping the police in their enquiries" it just *might* do you some good.'

'How the hell can I help you?' Wardman closed his eyes in despair.

'The weapon.'

'I don't know *where* the weapon is. I didn't *use* a weapon.'

'You just sat there and talked?'

Wardman remained silent.

'*Talked* him to death?'

'I keep telling you . . .'

'Both of you in the altogether?'

'If the mental picture pleases you.'

'You're not here to please me, sonny. You're here to explain certain irrefutable facts. That you were *there*. That bloody fingermarks were found on the shower curtain . . . *your* fingermarks. That blood was mixed with the water in the shower trap . . . his blood.'

Wardman wiped his mouth with the back of his hand.

'I don't need pleasing, sonny,' continued Belamy. 'I'm already highly delighted. I have you nailed, but good.'

Clarke listened and, albeit reluctantly, marvelled. Like toothpaste from a gently squeezed tube, an admission was very gradually being forced into the open. The amazement, therefore. That it could be done. More . . . that a man like Belamy could do it.

Clarke was a copper. A uniformed copper, and with only about half his service completed. But, nevertheless, he was wise in the ways of interrogation. Second-hand wise, of course. Occasionally the beat bobby had the opportunity to question a suspect about some fiddling little tin-pot crime, but the big stuff – the murder stakes – were reserved for C.I.D. and, moreover, for the top brass of C.I.D. Despite this restriction, he'd been witness at some sweet little sessions of interrogative technique, and by experts. And always – *always* – there'd been that first stage of mock-friendliness. The all-pals-together – I'm-doing-it-but-I'm-not-enjoying-doing-it – stage. No bish, bash, wallop antics. That (or so the theory went) merely drove the villain farther back into his knot-hole. The object was to tease a confession from him . . . but, again, the theory.

Belamy, on the other hand, had done zero teasing. He'd mocked. He'd snarled. He'd shouted. He'd threatened. He'd done all the wrong things, but he'd pulled it. As near as dammit.

Bluff?

Certainly some of it *had* to be bluff. Even Wardman had to be wise enough to see that. But bluff, built on bluff, built on more bluff. Christ, it was *working*.

In the time it had taken the car to travel a few hundred miles a flat denial had been changed into a near-confession. Lies had been told, then retracted. Other lies had been substituted, then *they'd* been retracted.

A core of lies, exposed by a web of bluff. There was only one ending. Either here in the car, or in the dock of Lessford Crown Court. Wardman was going down. A prison cell was already waiting.

And *Belamy* had done it!

Belamy was a bastard. No argument. No doubt. Known, recognised and tabulated as an unmitigated lout carrying some degree of authority. But he'd taken Wardman – a man who'd been threaded through the police machine before, therefore a man who should have known the score – and he'd skinned him and boned him, with little more than noise and bluster.

Okay, Wardman was a mug. That running away caper had *really* sealed the can. God help the barrister lumbered

100

with the job of explaining *that* one away. Add to which, all the fanny about ̶h̶e̶ him and Richardson sitting there, as God made them, chit-chatting about books and such.

Hell's teeth! (He glanced at the prisoner.) The man was a raving maniac.

Hoyle, on the other hand, was gradually feeling more and more confident. It was coming. Against all odds, it was *coming*. The accident had screwed things up, almost beyond repair. A break, and not a small break, in the pressure being applied to Wardman by Belamy. But the break had been bridged. Wardman's attempted escape had built that bridge . . . hence the confidence.

He allowed his mind to wander a little; to reach ahead to their destination and dwell upon the remarkable woman he'd married.

Alva Hoyle. *Doctor* Alva Hoyle. Would she approve?

Odd that a man who carried a detective chief inspectorship worried so much about the approval, or disapproval, of his wife. Odd that it should be so important. But it *was* important.

In all things Alva's blessing was necessary. What he was – the rank he'd reached – was a mere quirk in his own make-up. He could 'take' thieves. Thieves, murderers, rapists. He had the knack, and it was a God-given knack.

But Alva . . . Alva could have been *anything*. She, too, had a 'knack'. She soaked up knowledge with as much ease as a dry sponge soaked up water. Real knowledge. That doctorate. A pushover. A photographic memory, coupled with instant recall, coupled with the ability to *understand*. Tough subjects, too. Philosophy. Literature. Psychology. History. Language. Good God, she could have walked into just about any job going . . . and she'd plumped for being a copper's wife. And just that, too. No planned career of her own, just 'Mrs Hoyle'.

Great, except the pressure to keep abreast had at first

been almost killing. He (Hoyle) hadn't wanted to let *her* down. He'd yearned to talk and think on *her* level. Friend, that had been some task! He'd ploughed his way through books which had scared the hell out of him before he'd opened the covers.

And they'd had rows . . .

'David, forget it. Don't drive yourself crazy. Half that stuff you're reading is pure crap.'

'All right. It's crap. *You* say so.'

'Take my word, pet.'

'*I* want to know. I want to be able to understand it well enough to either agree or disagree. To make up my own mind.'

'You're a good copper. Be satisfied.'

'The hell for an excuse. I'm like two short planks alongside you.'

'So what do you want? A dumb blonde as a wife?'

'I want *you*.'

'You've *got* me.'

'I mean as an equal. To be *your* equal.'

'Menstrual cycle and all.'

'Don't be so damned stupid.'

'*You're* the stupid one. We're different. Accept it. We love each other, leave it at that.'

'You can make me feel a fool.'

'Do I? Ever?'

'No . . . but you *could*.'

'Einstein could make *me* look a fool. What do *I* care?'

'Man and wife. There's a hell of a diference.'

'It would be fine if you could make *me* look a fool, that it?'

'I wouldn't.'

'Now, there's a stupid thing to say.' The Welsh temper had slipped its moorings. 'All right, boy. I'm going out.'

'Where?'

'Some gymnasium. You concentrate on brains, I'll start

building up my biceps. We'll *really* be the same.'

'Alva, can't you see . . . ?'

'Oh, get lost!'

The Welsh temper and his own stiff-necked pride. Christ, they *must* have loved each other. Still did . . . but with a far deeper and more mature love. Instead of the scorching, flame-thrower heat of the past, it was now the steady, never-ending warmth of a peat fire. Comforting, but carrying its own subtle price-tag. Not to let the other down . . . ever. And more. Never to commit an act or be part of anything of which the other might disapprove. Their secret of course – it wouldn't do to let some of the coppers over whom he held authority know of this weakness – but even though a secret, ever-present.

And what he was tacitly a part of, as far as Wardman was concerned, might have caused her to frown. Might have. Oh, sure, she knew the broad outlines. She knew the objective. Just that she might not be happy about the *manner* of reaching that objective.

Therefore, while feeling confident, he worried a little. The two emotions were strange bedfellows. Policing. Making the law work; taking it from dry-as-dust statute books and case decisions and transforming it into more than high-sounding words. *Within* the law, and yet hidden. Disguised.

Dammit, she *had* to approve.

That, or concur to murder.

Wardman broke one of the silences which punctuated the journey. He spoke directly to Belamy.

'What about you?' he asked.

'What *about* me?' Belamy looked puzzled.

'The night of the murder. The night Richardson was killed.'

Belamy frowned.

'So far, *you've* asked all the questions.' Wardman's tone

was quiet. Polite enough. 'Why not answer a few?'

'I don't see what . . .'

'Where were *you*?'

'What the hell!'

'That file.' Wardman moved his head. Maybe it's genuine. Maybe it's not.'

'It's genuine, sonny. Lay your life on it.'

'That's exactly what you're asking me to do, but what if it's not?'

'Not?' Belamy's frown turned into a glare.

'What if it's all hokum? Claptrap?'

'Take my word . . .'

'Where does that leave you? Where does it leave *anybody*?'

'Those prints on the . . .'

'Just your say-so. How do *I* know?'

'We don't do things . . .'

'You "do things" to get a conviction, sergeant.' The smile was a little sad. 'Anything. It's stopped being a gentleman's game . . . if it ever was. That's why I'm asking – out of curiosity of course – did *you* kill Clive Richardson?'

'Of all the bloody . . .'

'Can you *prove* you didn't?'

'Wardman, I'm warning you. Any more . . .'

'A question,' said Wardman mildly. 'I'm innocent – as innocent as you claim to be – until and unless a jury find otherwise. As one innocent man to another, *did* you kill him?'

'Five minutes with you, sonny.' Belamy's tone was a soft, snarling growl. 'Just five minutes, alone and in a locked room. I'd damn soon . . .'

'That would be proof of your aggression, not proof of your innocence.'

In the front passenger seat Hoyle listened with growing amazement and not a little amusement. The biter was being bit, and the biter wasn't enjoying the experience. It was hopeless, of course, but it was a novel approach.

Something Belamy hadn't expected, and something which had come up at him like a brick wall. It would be interesting – very interesting – to hear his reaction.

Wardman was saying, 'You say I visited him on the night of his murder and if that file is genuine – even part-genuine – you can prove it. I admit it. I visited him. But I wasn't the only visitor. His murderer, too, visited him . . .'

'You're the murderer, sonny.'

'. . . and that could be *anybody*. You, for example. Anybody! Anybody who can't prove they *didn't* murder him. That's the way you work, sergeant. The wrong way, but *your* way. You don't detect crime. You detect criminals – one specific criminal – then you fit him out with some undetected crime he *might* have committed. Like ready-made suits, off a peg.

'But think about it. Some of those suits could fit *you*. This one, for example. Where *were* you when Richardson was battered to death? Because nobody saw you enter and leave, that doesn't mean you *didn't* enter and leave. Who can give you a hundred per-cent . . .'

'*Hold it right there!*'

The explosion came, and for a moment it seemed as if Belamy was going to attack Wardman there in the rear of the car.

Hoyle half-turned and rapped, '*You* hold it, sergeant. Words, that's all. A goading. Can't you see that?'

Wardman was smiling, as if at a private joke.

'A goading,' he admitted gently. 'A demonstration. Two can play that game.'

And yet . . . and yet . . .

Clarke could feel it, like a small electric current reaching him through the steel of the handcuffs. A last desperate throw. A final attempt at steering Belamy away from that point beyond which there was no return. On the face of it – the carrying of the battle into the camp of the enemy – Wardman gave the impression of being a man without real fear. But it was a façade. A bluff and a last bluff . . . and it came through.

Goading?

Or perhaps the final defiance, like the last pawing of the ground by a fighting bull before he lowered his head and waited for the sword.

It earned a respite.

The motor patrol sergeant turned into the service area between junctions thirty and thirty-one. Hoyle took over the wheel and, other than halting the Cortina long enough for them to change seats, that was it. Nobody had spoken and no time was wasted. Hoyle eased the car from the service area and into the stream of traffic driving north along the motorway.

The day was at last closing its eyes. Dusk. The most dangerous period of all for driving. The eyes have not yet accustomed themselves; night vision is not yet here, indeed is not yet needed. But daylight is going fast and (always!) some damn fools are already driving on full headlights which, if not coming towards you, are being reflected in the driving mirrors.

'Easy for a few miles, sir,' murmured the motor patrol sergeant.

Hoyle grunted acknowledgement of the advice.

The 'sir' had come out quite naturally. They were nearing home ground. Rank was coming into its own. Strange how it happened; down south they'd been four men sharing a particularly tiring job; now – very gradually – they were becoming a chief inspector, two sergeants and a constable each performing their respective duty, complete with authority and responsibility. And moreover weariness was tightening like a closing clamp. The throb of the engine. The confines of the car. The never-ending motorway. The everlasting rush and surge of other vehicles. Like a mad fairground ride which never stopped and they couldn't leave.

Clarke lighted a cigarette. It was awkward; the handcuffed left wrist prevented movement without also raising and lowering Wardman's right hand. The smoke from the cigarette tasted sour and harsh. With the first inhalation he wished he hadn't lit the damn thing.

'Not too far now.' Belamy turned his head and gazed at the darkening landscape. Then to Wardman, and in a low, threatening tone, 'You'll soon be in an interview room, sonny. You'll sing a different tune there.'

'I didn't kill him.'

There was no real emotion in the denial. The impression was that he'd long tired of mouthing the words, but self-preservation required them to be repeated over and over again.

Belamy lifted the file from its place in the door-pocket, placed it on his knee and, although it was no longer light enough to read the contents, he fingered the pages as if reminding himself.

He intoned, 'Witnesses. You were seen going. You were seen coming away. No argument on that score. You were there and at the right time. You say you spent the rest of the night in your car. Who'll believe that? Bordfield. Lessford. Plenty of places. Plenty of beds. You stripped off completely. Showered. Talked – that's what *you* say. Two men, naked, talking to each other. Two known queens. Just *talking*. Who'll believe *that*?'

Wardman raised his free hand and gently touched the swelling on his cheek. Clarke could feel the slight shudder as Belamy continued the litany.

'Fingerprints. *Your* fingerprints. Bloody. On the shower curtain. Blood in the shower trap. Richardson's blood group. The fingerprints . . . Richardson's blood group. You had a shower. That much you admit. The rest? Who'll believe? Which jury won't convict? You make a run for it. Why? Innocence?'

'Fear,' muttered Wardman.

'Guilt . . . it has to be guilt.'

'Four policemen. One of them a man like you.'

'Like *me*?' Belamy sounded genuinely surprised. Genuinely puzzled. 'I'm no different.'

'Judge, jury . . . executioner,' breathed Wardman.

'I do a job. It's what I'm paid for.'

'It's *how* you do it.'

'My way. I've never put an innocent man inside.'

'No?' Wardman's lips curved into a sardonic smile.

'Not knowingly.'

'In that case, I'll be the first.'

'I can't help you, sonny.' Perhaps the hint of sorrow was real. Perhaps it was a put-on. Only Belamy knew.

'Help me?' The smile stayed on Wardman's lips.

'Tell the court that *you* helped *us*.'

'How?'

'The weapon. We haven't found the weapon.'

'I don't know where the weapon is.'

'Or even what it was. If you've destroyed it . . .'

'I don't know what it was.'

'One day you'll wish you had,' sighed Belamy.

'What?'

'Helped. Come clean.'

'Helped *you*?'

'Helped yourself. Given us something we could have told the court. Something in your favour.'

'I didn't kill him.' Then the pause and the soft, almost throw-away addendum. 'He was dead when I arrived.'

SIX

Something about 'They also serve'. One more thing the writers of flash crime novels rarely touch upon. The wives and *their* worry.

Helen Flensing said, 'When he came – the second time he came – he was too concerned about the delay. The interruption. The accident – I mean, the fact that there'd *been* an accident – was secondary.'

'Look, my pet.' Alva was still there. She didn't mind; it was more than a duty but, no denying the fact, somebody with an iron lung wrapped around them had cause for spats of self-pity, and Helen Flensing couldn't quite fight this one off. 'Ralph came and told you. As I understand things, my old man had asked somebody at the scene of the snarl-up to make contact. Nothing specific. Just to warn of the delay. Then when they reached a pub, David phoned in more details, Ralph telephoned me and I trotted along to tell *you*. You're in the picture, my love. Nobody's holding anything back.'

Alva switched on the light against the thickening darkness, then flipped the curtains across the window.

'Like a cell, isn't it?' Helen moved her head from side to side.

'What?'

'This place. About the right size. White, too. Cells are often white, but the prisoner can move around. Walk about. Look out of the . . .'

'You'd prefer a sink, would you?' Alva's tone carried no hint of sympathy. 'A sink. Four or five snotty-nosed kids, yelling and bawling around the house all day. Nappies to wash. Bottoms to wipe. All the washing up – all the cleaning – all the muck and mess of kids' diseases. Not white, mark you. Black would be nearer the mark. And a hubby fed up to the back teeth with your complaining. Beds to make. Meals to prepare. All the dreary . . .'

'Shut up!' Helen's lip began to tremble. 'You have a choice. You *can* do it. If you don't feel like . . .'

'I still have to do it, girl. I've the same choice as you, no choice at all.' There was a pause, then, 'This is one of your days, my love. Fine. A woman's prerogative. Just get it all out of your system, see? Throw it at me. I'll understand. I'll fight back. Give you somebody to argue with. Just don't – y'know – leave it for the menfolk. They *don't* understand. You'll hurt them. You'll hurt Ralph, and he *won't* fight back.'

'You're fond of Ralph.' There was just the hint of accusation in the words.

'Fond of Ralph. Fond of you. Fond of a handful of people.'

'Maybe a little too fond.'

'My lovely.' Alva's eyes flashed. 'You make that suggestion once more and, upright *or* horizontal, you'll feel the weight of my hand.'

Hoyle eased the Cortina onto the hard shoulder of the motorway, and braked to a halt. It was a small but necessary illegality. The questioning of Wardman had reached a point beyond which it was dangerous to allow Belamy to go. The detective sergeant had done his job. The softening up process was complete. The big stick had to be exchanged for the scalpel.

Hoyle opened the door gingerly; traffic coming up on the slow lane of the motorway roared past with not much more than a yard to spare. He spoke to the motor patrol sergeant.

'Move over, sergeant. It's yours for the rest of the way.'

'Yes, sir.'

The motor patrol sergeant negotiated the gear-stick and hand brake and took over the driving seat without leaving the car.

Hoyle walked round the car and opened the rear nearside door.

'Take over the front seat, Belamy.'

'Look, if you think . . .'

'The front seat,' snapped Hoyle. 'This is where you bow out for a while.'

'Flensing said . . .'

'*Chief Superintendent* Flensing.' The tone and the facial expression slapped Belamy into his niche. 'Nobody's nicking the case from you. Let's say you've justified *your* existence. It's time I justified mine.'

'My case,' muttered Belamy.

'Your case.' Hoyle's voice was quiet, but convincing. 'In the interview room he's all yours. Till then *I* talk . . . now into the front seat, sergeant, we've wasted enough time.'

Belamy climbed from the car and took over the seat alongside the motor patrol sergeant. The motor patrol sergeant checked that Hoyle was safely alongside Wardman, then moved into the flow of traffic. He forced himself to concentrate upon driving; it was necessary, if only to keep his mind occupied. This (he'd thought) was going to be an easy number. Drive south, then back home again. Dead safe. Dead cushy. Christ . . . it was like handling a time bomb on wheels.

Flensing, too, was feeling the growing tension. The limb was lonely and (was it imagination?) the tree seemed to be swaying slightly. He wasn't given to seeing omens, but news of the accident had not been good news. The thing had to be done smoothly and the accident *must* have caused

111

at least a hiccup. In spirit, he was miles away, in the Cortina. Knowing – *hoping* – that the build-up in atmosphere within the confines of the car was having the desired effect.

Frightening . . . but more than frightening. Far more than merely frightening.

To frighten a man was easy. To frighten a *guilty* man was like taking toffee from a child. Any copper with half-a-dozen years' service under his belt could do that, no sweat. But then what? After the fear? Don't let him get used to the fear. Don't let him learn to live with it. Frighten the bastard, then push it. No plateau upon which he could rest. No easing up while he got a second wind.

Push him, David. Keep pushing. You know how. You know what's needed. Don't let Belamy go too far. For God's sake, time it properly. Time it to the second. You're not Belamy, old son. You know things the Belamys of this world will never know. That a man – every man – has a conscience. Let Belamy scare him – let Belamy scare the daylights out of him – but that's all. Know when to take over . . . *please*. Know when to pull the con. Know when to slap Belamy down, and push fear beyond just fear. Fear . . . plus. Make the confession come out of him. Out of his pores, if necessary.

Get it, David. For God's sake, *get it*!

He left his office and wandered along neon-lit corridors until he reached the main C.I.D. Room. A large room. Standard. Desks, filing cabinets and telephones; charts, rotas and calendars fastened to the walls. The official 'justification'. The paperwork. Not where it was 'done', but where it was 'recorded'.

Two detective constables stood up as he entered. One placed a half-smoked cigarette on the lip of an ash-tray.

'Who's on night-duty stand-by?'

Flensing's voice was its usual quiet drawl. Not a trace of the turmoil boiling around inside his brain.

'I am, sir.' The cigarette-smoker spoke, then, as Flensing

112

raised polite, questioning eyebrows, 'Detective Constable Shaw, sir.'

'Everything quiet, Shaw?'

'Yes, sir, so far.'

'Hold yourself in readiness, please.'

'Sir?' Shaw looked puzzled.

'Anything a beat constable can handle, let him. Stay here where I can contact you. I may want you later.'

'Yes, sir.' Shaw hesitated, then added, 'What if something big comes up, sir?'

'Contact me personally. Don't leave the building without my permission. Understood?'

'Yes, sir, understood.'

Flensing smiled, nodded, left the C.I.D. Room and returned to his own office.

They'd moved from the M1 to the M18. Soon they'd be on the A1. Dual-carriageway, but not motorway. M18 onto the A1(M) and from there to the A1. And from there north . . . and home.

It was dark now. Dark, with pinpoint stars showing whenever the sky was visible. But dark like a gloomy disco, with the flash and pass of headlights from approaching and overtaking vehicles; a near-hypnotic flickering of lights which added to the overall bone-weariness of those in the car.

Hoyle lighted a cigarette, and for a moment the three occupants of the rear seat seemed to be picked out in the orange-coloured flame of the lighter. Travel-tiredness etched lines on their faces, and the lighter flame accentuated the shadows. Hoyle smoked a quarter of the cigarette in silence, then when he spoke it was in a reasonable tone. The tone of a man anxious to understand.

'You haven't helped yourself, Wardman.'

'No.' Wardman stared ahead and spoke the single word in a soft expression of hopeless near-capitulation.

'That rather ridiculous statement about having a shower because you felt grubby, then the two of you sitting in the nude holding a meaningless conversation.'

Wardman nodded.

'That wouldn't have gone down too well in court, would it?'

'No.'

'And now this.'

'He *was* dead when I arrived,' groaned Wardman.

'If you hadn't told so many lies before . . .'

Hoyle left the sentence unfinished. It was a mere pointing out. A reminding. He left it at that, and the silence stretched out into seconds . . . then minutes.

At last Wardman breathed, 'He *was* dead,' and it sounded almost like an echo of his previous words.

'In which case,' said Hoyle gently, 'you should have telephoned the police.'

Wardman nodded dumbly.

'Why the shower?' asked Hoyle. 'You did take a shower?'

'Blood.' Wardman shivered, as if touched by a sudden blast of cold air. 'Blood everywhere.'

'I know . . . we saw him.'

'Everywhere.' Wardman gave the appearance of voicing his own thoughts. His memories. Terrible memories. He stared ahead as he spoke. 'I didn't know . . . didn't realise. So much blood in one person. Everywhere! I – I tried to turn him over. Tried to lift him. But – but my hand slipped. Blood, you see. He wasn't dead. I didn't believe he was dead. *Couldn't* believe.' Slow tears spilled and trickled down his face. 'But he *was*. I talked to him . . . but he was dead. His skull. His face. Clive, oh, Clive. He was – he was . . .'

The voice trailed off, but the tears continued.

Hoyle smoked his cigarette and left Wardman to live out his misery. Clarke could feel the sobs, silent and half-controlled, but he could feel them. In the front seats Belamy stared stone-faced along the lines of the dipped

114

headlights. The motor patrol sergeant gripped and relaxed his fingers on the steering wheel in a steady rhythm; this was detection – 'crime detection' – and it was getting at him. It was foul. Worse than any road accident. More terrifying. Worse and very deliberate. To take a grown man and chop him up – heart, soul, mind, everything – then watch him suffer and not even show sympathy.

The motor patrol sergeant eased his foot down a little. The car gathered speed.

Home, for God's sake. Home and sanity.

The cadet tapped on the door. Flensing called, 'Come,' the cadet entered Flensing's office and carefully placed the tray with the beaker of tea and plate of biscuits on the desk.

'Thanks,' said Flensing then, as the cadet turned to leave, 'You're on late, youngster.'

'Yes, sir.' The cadet grinned. 'All night, sir. It gets us used to working irregular hours.'

'That's the theory?'

'We're not allowed on the streets, sir.'

'I should think not.'

'I think we should be, sir.' The cadet became a little bolder.

'Why?' smiled Flensing.

'Experience, sir. It will make us better officers.'

'*When* you're officers,' added Flensing.

'Yes sir.'

Flensing broke a biscuit into two halves, then asked, 'Why, son?'

'Sir?'

'The force – this force, any force – what made you join? Why want to be a copper?'

'It's a fine job, sir.'

'Just for the moment forget the rank, son.' Flensing popped a piece of biscuit into his mouth. 'Don't trot out the expected answers. The truth . . . what made you join?'

'My father's a sergeant, sir.'

'This force?'

'No, sir. London.'

'And he didn't try to dissuade you?'

'He – er – he wasn't keen, sir.'

'No,' mused Flensing, 'he wouldn't be. But he couldn't put you off, eh?'

'I met him half-way.' The cadet was enjoying this quiet chinwag with a higher-up. 'I didn't join the Met.'

'A good force the Met,' drawled Flensing.

'Second best, sir.'

'Your father might not agree, of course.'

'He's biased.'

'And you're *not*?'

'My mother's a Yorkshirewoman, sir.'

'Ah!'

'She's quite pleased.'

'Yes, she would be.' Flensing sipped tea, replaced the beaker onto the tray, then said, 'Thank you, son. Come back for the empties in about half an hour.'

'Yes, sir. Thank you, sir.'

Flensing stared at the closed door and munched biscuit and sipped tea. A nice kid. The sort of kid he'd like for a son. The sort he'd have *liked* for a son. Sure of himself, without being cocky. Knowing where politeness ended and lickspittle began. The sort of son he'd have liked. Guts enough to oppose his father, but obedient enough to meet him half-way.

The father?

A sergeant in the Met. Uniformed or C.I.D.? It didn't matter. That barrel held a lot of apples and some were rotten. Some of the big apples were rotten. But not the cadet's father, that at an educated guess. Bent coppers make lousy parents. No. That boy's old man was with the majority. The sound fruit made suspect by those with grubs in their guts.

116

So, in time, he'd make a good copper. Bet on *that*, too. A good copper and a disillusioned man. The two went together. The disillusionment was part of the experience, and the experience made the cop.

Policing. Fatherhood. Marriage. His mind flipped and skirted memories and possibilities . . . *and* impossibilities. Sure they'd had rows. He and Helen. When she'd been whole; before she'd been smashed up and placed in a position where no decent man – no decent husband – could show other than love and understanding. Some monumental rows.

'Mr Everret once told me. "I warned you not to marry him" . . .'

Who the hell was Mr Everret? Some pillock eager to drop pearls of marital wisdom in a young wife's ear. Other than that Flensing couldn't put a face to the name. Not a face, but a character. The sort of jumped-up little popinjay, old enough to know better, but with an eye to a neat figure.

She'd blurted it out and there'd been one hell of a row. Why hadn't she taken Mr Everret's advice? Why hadn't she allowed the knowledgeable Mr Everret to choose the mug she must marry? Why waste time thinking things out for herself when the all-wise Mr Everret was at hand to give guidance? Come to that who had Mr bloody Everret had in mind?

That had been one of the big ones. One of those rows well worth remembering. They'd each used their tongues like stock-whips. Lashing and hurting and, moreover, *wanting* to hurt. But the *reason* for the row? The tiny insignificant spark which had triggered off the great Everret explosion. Damned if he could remember *that*. Like all rows and every row. That one step too far . . . *that* had been the launch pad.

The memories jostled for position. Good memories and bad memories. But all of them part of a married life. *Normal* married life.

Dear God, why couldn't they row any more? Why this

117

flat, uninteresting landscape, without hills and without
hollows? He loved her – dammit he worshipped her – but at
least let it have some sort of variety. Otherwise it would
wither. Otherwise it would grow to mean damn-all. That
infernal iron lung had turned her into a prissy-prissy
creature; had squeezed the fight out of her; had . . .

'Damn and blast it!'

Flensing made the effort and forced the dark mood from
himself. This waiting. This wondering. This worrying. This
bloody *case*!

He popped the last of the biscuits into his mouth, drained
the beaker and stood up. He needed air and exercise. There
wasn't a thing he could do to help.

'Did you love him?'

Hoyle asked the question quietly and with sincerity. It
was the sort of question Belamy could never have asked.

'What?' Wardman raised puzzled, red-rimmed eyes.

'Richardson. Did you love him? Did he love you'

'Good Lord, no.' It was a soft, bitter answer. 'Nobody
could love Clive. He was too selfish.'

'You had a key.'

'So had other people.'

'He just . . .' Hoyle hesitated, then ended, 'gave keys.'

'His way. He was a male whore. You paid . . . cash or
kind.'

'And – you *now* say – he was dead when you arrived?'

Wardman moved his head in a single nod.

'Messy?'

'Great heavens, you *saw* him. You must have . . .'

'Of course I saw him,' soothed Hoyle.

'In that case . . .'

'What I'm wondering is,' Hoyle paused, then murmured,
'So obviously dead. So obviously *murdered*. Why touch him?
Why turn him over?'

'I didn't turn him over. I only *tried* to turn him over.'

'Okay, why try?'

'He was . . .' Wardman tried to move his hands, but the handcuffs prevented free movement. 'He might *not* have been dead.'

'Come *on!*' It was gently smiling derision.

'I'm not an expert,' muttered Wardman.

'You seriously thought he might be alive?'

'It – it seemed possible.'

'With the back of his skull caved in? With half his brain hung out?'

'Stop it!'

'The hell I'll stop it, I want the truth.'

'Yes. I thought he might still be alive. I *hoped* he was still alive. I *wanted* him to be alive.' Wardman gabbled the words then, in a whisper, 'Who wants anybody to die that way?'

'Somebody,' said Hoyle flatly.

'And you think me?'

'Not "wanted".' Hoyle chose his words carefully. 'Shall we say *did* . . . without realising.'

'Why *me?*' pleaded Wardman.

'You were there. Why *not* you?'

'Only *that?*' His lip curled and there was the hint of outrage in his tone.

'And a few other things,' said Hoyle softly.

'The shower? My God! I keep telling you . . . the blood. It was everywhere. On my hands, on my clothes, even in my hair. I had to get it off. I couldn't . . .' He had to pause for breath. The outburst seemed to fill the speeding car; to drown the noise of passing traffic. The wild desire to be believed exploded the words from his mouth. 'God dammit! Understand. Try to understand. *Try.* I had to wash – to shower – to get the blood off me. People don't think. In those circumstances, people don't stop to think. Clive was dead and I was messed up. I – I undressed and showered. Tried to clean as much from my clothes as possible. That's

119

all. That's all I did. I wanted to get out of there. I was . . .'

'Why?' The question stemmed the flow.

'Why what?'

'Why did you "want to get out of there"?'

'Are you crazy? A dead man – a *murdered* man –'

'I visited the scene. Saw him. Stayed quite a while. *I* didn't need a shower to get the blood off.'

'For Christ's sake!'

'Why did you?'

'I've told you. I touched him. I thought . . .'

'Personally, I had no doubts. He was dead. Very dead.'

'I suppose . . .' Wardman swallowed. 'Wishful thinking.'

'You wanted him alive?'

'Of course.'

'Why?'

'Good God, I knew him. I didn't want *anybody* . . .'

'On the problematic – the *very* problematic – assumption that you didn't kill him . . .'

'I keep telling you . . .'

'. . . why didn't you telephone the police?'

'I – I . . .'

'He was in the bedroom?'

'Yes.'

'There was a telephone in the bedroom?'

Wardman nodded.

Hoyle said, 'Step at a time, please. Before we go any further. Why didn't you telephone the police?'

After the heat of the day, the night air had a chill to it. Stars galore and a moon in its first quarter and polished like a well-kept scimitar blade. Flensing pulled the collar of his jacket up against the touch of goose-flesh, thrust his hands into the pockets of his trousers and strolled along the narrow path which crossed and re-crossed the formal lawn and rose beds which formed the apron to the frontage of Lessford Regional Headquarters.

120

Everything neat. Everything tidy. The rose beds clean of weeds, the grass closely mown, up there in the heavens every star in its allotted position and the moon exactly where it should be.

It was nice to remember that. Comforting. Proof that not quite *everything* was screwed up to hell and beyond.

Not that Flensing was sure, of course. Just a feeling. A suspicion. Much like being the member of an audience watching a stage magician sawing some flashy young lady in half; having the feeling that the saw wasn't *really* separating her boobs from her backside and, for her sake, hoping you were right. That sort of a feeling. A feeling which amounted to a certainty . . . almost.

Only this time in reverse.

Playing patsy with parlour psychology was a mug's game. *That* saw (figuratively speaking) had teeth. *That* trick couldn't be pulled.

In a murder enquiry you either had evidence, or you did *not* have evidence. Evidence enough to convict. That or nothing. To 'know' wasn't enough. To be 99.9% certain meant nothing. Forget that .1% – forget the evidence it represented – and a man who'd committed murder walked free.

'Why didn't you telephone the police?' repeated Hoyle.

'I was terrified,' muttered Wardman.

'Of what?'

'Of the situation. Of *this*.'

'An innocent man would have telephoned the police,' insisted Hoyle.

Wardman shook his head slowly. The despair was absolute.

'All right,' continued Hoyle. 'Let's take it as you're now telling it. You saw the body, you touched it, you cleaned yourself under the shower. What then?'

'I left.'

'For where?'

'The car. I'd parked my car. I sat there – oh, I don't know how long. Trembling.'

'In wet clothes?' asked Hoyle quietly.

'What?'

'You tried to clean the blood from your clothes, remember? With water, presumably.'

'They were . . . damp. Not properly clean.'

'But you sat in them?'

'Yes. Of course.'

'In the car?'

Wardman nodded.

'Where was the car parked?' asked Hoyle.

'In a park. Near Richardson's place.'

'Not on the street.'

'No.'

'Other cars on the park?'

'I think so. A lorry. I remember a lorry.'

'How far from Richardson's home?'

'Oh, about a hundred yards. Maybe more.'

'You knew of it, of course?'

'What?'

'This car park? You didn't have to *find* it?'

'I'd – I'd used it before, yes.'

'How many times?'

'Oh, I don't know. Three or four times. Maybe more.'

'And you just sat there?'

Wardman nodded.

'Why not drive away immediately? Why wait?'

'I was frightened.'

'Therefore, why *not* drive away? You were frightened, why not put as much distance as possible between yourself and what had frightened you as quickly as possible?'

'I was in a state.'

'Why?'

'Heavens above, man, I'd just left . . .'

'But – if you're to be believed – you hadn't killed him.'

Wardman remained silent.

Hoyle continued, 'You found a body. A murder victim. Murder victims *are* found . . . almost always. People don't run away. Not if they're innocent. They notify the police. You didn't.'

'You're twisting my words,' breathed Wardman.

'*Are* you innocent?' asked Hoyle flatly.

'Of course. I've said so I don't know how many . . .'

'And if you're not?'

Wardman frowned.

'Would you admit it?' teased Hoyle.

'I – I suppose not.'

'You see where we stand?' smiled Hoyle.

'That's what I did,' groaned Wardman. 'I ran from the house, then sat in the car. Then drove away. I'm not a hero. I was frightened.'

'But not frightened enough to drive away . . . *immediately*?'

'It's what I did. Take it or leave it.'

The balancing act. That's what it amounted to; an immaculately performed balancing act. There was an admission coming . . . that or the whole exercise had been a waste of time. But in order to retain the balance it was vital that movement be continued. Movement of some sort. Not to create a situation where Wardman had to fight back; if he fought back movement would cease. The *initiative* had to stay with Hoyle. It was a questioning – an interrogation – not an argument. Argument pre-supposed doubt. Doubt on one side, doubt on the other, doubt on both sides. *There was no doubt*. Arguments equated with compromises . . . and there couldn't be a compromise.

Hoyle said, 'All right, we'll "take it". We'll accept it at its face value . . . for what that's worth. You eventually drove off. Where to?'

'Home.'

'Home?' It was a combined question and exclamation. 'From Lessford to the south coast?'

'That's where I live.'

'A long way,' observed Hoyle. 'A very long way.'

'I stopped, telephoned in, told them I was sick, then continued home.'

'You'd have to re-fuel.'

'Of course. I stayed on the A1. I used a self-service station.'

'Which one?'

'I don't know. I didn't notice. Just the one.'

'Meals?'

'I didn't stop for a meal.'

'Just . . . home? Straight home?'

'Yes.'

'An uncommon amount of panic,' mused Hoyle.

Wardman made no comment.

'For an innocent man,' added Hoyle.

'*You* say I'm guilty.'

Hoyle ignored the remark and said, 'You live alone.'

'You know I do.'

'When you arrived home, what then?'

'I bathed.' He hesitated, then added, 'Then I burned my clothes.'

'Ah!'

'They were soiled.'

'They were also evidence,' murmured Hoyle.

'Evidence of *what*?'

'Of blood-stains. Richardson's blood. Evidence that you'd *been* there . . .'

'I've already admitted . . .'

'Ah, yes. *Now*. But *then*. The last thing you wanted was evidence that you'd been anywhere near Richardson's body. Burn the clothes . . . where's the connection?'

124

'You're twisting things,' muttered Wardman.

'I'm twisting nothing,' said Hoyle coldly. 'I'm getting at part of the truth. Not all of it, but some. The twisting – the dodging and the turning – that, so far, has been *your* mode of action. Lies based upon more lies.' He stared through the gloom and into Wardman's eyes. 'The unvarnished truth. However foul. However disgusting. That will satisfy me . . . and nothing less.'

It was a little like being linked to a shuddering volcano. That or feeling the first warning tremors of an earthquake. Maybe the handcuffs and the nearness of the man. Whatever, Clarke felt it.

It was a terrible feeling. No joy. No jubilation. Not even satisfaction that a murderer was on the point of admitting his guilt.

A terrible feeling. More . . . a *terrifying* feeling.

One man against a machine. He hadn't a chance. The police machine, complete with forensic science, limitless man-hours, as many men as the enquiry demanded, the near-art of fingerprint identification, a bottomless purse and an organisation which covered every square inch of the United Kingdom, and if necessary beyond. All that, versus one man.

He was going to crash. He *had* to crash.

The knowledge gave Clarke a deep-down sadness.

'Why won't you believe me?' pleaded Wardman.

'Which version?' taunted Hoyle gently. 'The sitting-down-and-talking version? The visiting-an-old-friend version? The-sitting-in-the-car-after-having-been-rejected version? Pick the version you want me to believe. I won't make promises, but we'll concentrate on *that* version.'

'I – I've lied.'

'Oh, boy!'

'I'm sorry.'

'You've also tried to escape. Talk *that* one away.'

'I – I was scared.'

'Scared. Always scared. Wardman – believe me – innocent men are *not* scared. Not to the extent you're scared. If they're caught in compromising situations, they're uncomfortable. Maybe a little ashamed. They waffle around a little until they see sense. The frightened ones are the guilty ones . . . always.'

'You think I'm guilty. You *still* think I'm guilty.'

'I *know* you're guilty.' Hoyle's tone of voice carried no hint of doubt. No hatred, no contempt, not even dislike. But, nevertheless, not a hint of doubt. He continued, 'It's why you were picked up. It's why we've travelled hundreds of miles to bring you back to where you belong. You've already cost the rate-payers of Lessford a lot of money, Wardman. Guilty? You're as guilty as hell . . . and you know it.'

Wardman sighed. Deep and long. A shuddering sigh of defeat.

Hoyle said, 'To put it in simple language, Wardman. We can place you at the scene of the crime, at the *time* of the crime. We can prove that your hands were covered in blood. *Richardson's* blood. All that crap about having left him after your little talk . . .'

'I've already said . . .'

'. . . It's all been noted. Evidence. Evidence of lies. Then the change of direction. Evidence of more lies. Lies, lies, lies. Wardman, you don't know *what* you've done. The realisation will come – *might* come – some months from now. When you're in prison. When you have time to think things out. A detective chief inspector, a detective sergeant, a uniformed sergeant, a uniformed constable. *We* don't have to lie. We don't even have to exaggerate. We merely follow each other into a witness box, tell the simple truth, and *your* lies will put you where you deserve to be. The finest barrister in the world. He hasn't a case. *You* haven't a case. Those twelve jury members *have* to reach the right verdict.'

Belamy was being give a lesson in interrogation and, to his credit, he had the sense to realise it. It wasn't *his* brand of interrogation. His brand was the crash-bang-wallop style, and until now he'd thought that was the only style. He was learning. The text books – what few text books had been written on the subject – all insisted upon a rapport between the interviewer and the interviewee; a sort of give-and-take approach which, theoretically, ended up with each man holding grudging respect for the other. Belamy had long thrown *that* theory onto the council tip. Belamy figured – *had* figured – that the verbal equivalent of the thumb-screw and the rack brought home the groceries; that anything less – anything else – was a waste of everybody's time.

Not so!

Hoyle was showing a third way. A gentle, quietly-spoken 'water torture' way. No shouting. No ranting. No threatening. Just keep talking ... and talking ... and talking. Having reached a point – a point where the man interrogated had told enough lies – take those lies and string them into a gentle monologue of never-ending accusation. Leave no gaps in which he can insert denials. Brick by brick, word by word, lie by lie, build a wall around him. A wall of his own making. A prison without doors or windows.

Wardman would eventually scream to be let out. He must! It was his only way of escape.

Belamy gnawed at his lower lip and stared through the windscreen, without consciously seeing the road ahead. He wasn't enjoying himself. He wasn't enjoying himself one bit. He'd been so sure. So sure ... and so *wrong*. That bloody poofty in the rear seat had seemed so soft. Soft as milk pudding. But he wasn't. No way! He'd taken all the pummelling he (Belamy) had been able to throw at him,

127

and had still come up for more.

But now . . .

Belamy frowned and wondered where it was going to
end. No, *how* it was going to end. Just *how*.

Things were happening inside Belamy's mind. Things he
didn't like, but things he'd no control over.

SEVEN

The A1(M) stretch was notorious for collecting fog. It sliced through industrial Yorkshire to the west of Doncaster, linking the motorway system to the A1 and, via some geographical quirk, attracted the spew from factories and power stations and, sometimes when every other stretch of motorway was clear as a bell, settled a hell's brew of grey/green muck in the path of speeding vehicles. A dozen miles of it, with more crashes per mile than any other road in the United Kingdom.

The motor patrol sergeant sent up a silent prayer. He was tired. The Cortina was built for long journeys, but even the Cortina – or if not the car the driver – had limits. The throbbing hum of the engine seemed to penetrate his hands through the steering wheel, to penetrate the soles of his feet through the pedals, and thereafter bounce from the inside of his skull. The stroboscopic flash of passing headlights. The monotonous hiss of road noise. The continued restriction of the seat belt. Everything!

God, let that stretch of the A1(M) stay clear of fog.

He'd crack. For sure he'd crack if they ran into a wall of fog. Behind him Hoyle wouldn't stop talking. Talk, talk, talk. Pile-driving the evidence into the mush of Wardman's brain; into the mush of the motor patrol sergeant's brain.

'Sit in that jury box, Wardman. Be a member of that jury. Nothing special. An ordinary man – an ordinary woman –

listening and knowing what everybody else knows. It's not sudden. It's weeks old. Television. Radio. Newspapers. The sort of murder that catches the headlines. A homosexual battered to death. All the gory details. The when, the where, the how. Nationwide coverage. And – if you're to be believed – *you found the body*.

'If you're to be believed!

'But who the hell's going to believe you? Who? An innocent man finds a murder victim. He mauls it around. It's obviously dead . . . *obviously* dead. Blood and muck all over the place. But for some reason best known to himself, he mauls it around. Gets himself blathered in gore. Gets his clothes messed up. Then quietly has a shower. He doesn't call the police. There's a telephone there in the room. All he has to do is lift the receiver and dial nine-nine-nine. That's all it needs. But, instead, he mauls the mutilated body around, then showers, dresses and leaves.

'*An innocent man*?

'Then there's the news coverage. Television, radio, headlines in all the nationals. The "murder of the month". He *has* to know it. He *has* to know the police want as much help as possible. He can't *not* know. But what does he do? He sits tight. He doesn't say a damn word . . . this "innocent" man. Even now he could telephone. Even now he could walk into any police station in the country – stop any copper on the street – and say, "That man, murdered in Lessford. I knew him. He was my friend. I visited him on the night he was murdered. He was dead. I didn't kill him, but I can pin-point the time of his death a little more accurately." He can still act normally. A little late. A little explaining to do. But if his story is true, it can be checked out and he'll be believed. He'll even be thanked for assisting the police . . . this "innocent" man.

'That jury – the men and women in that jury – they'd understand. They'd give him the benefit of the doubt. Weakness. Panic. But when he's pulled himself together, he

130

does the right thing.

'But, instead, what *does* he do? He holes up in a corner. He doesn't say a damn dicky-bird to a soul. He even burns the clothes he was wearing. This "innocent" man . . .'

'Ring them up,' suggested Helen. 'Ask them to let us know when they arrive at headquarters. Stay with me until then. Please.'

Alva nodded agreement.

The truth was, Alva was having to sit tight upon her impatience. She liked – indeed, she *loved* – Helen Flensing, but at the present moment she was finding that lady a pain in the neck. Okay, anybody condemned to live in an iron lung hadn't much to chuckle about, but Christ there was a limit. Sure, all women had their off days, but the trick was to fight a way to the surface, not try to pull everybody else under. And the truth was Helen had been more than a little trying.

Alva said, 'We'll have a fag first.'

'Don't you think . . . ?'

'I think, my pet,' said Alva calmly, 'that it is high time you grabbed yourself by the scruff of the neck and shook some sense into yourself.'

'Oh!'

'Have a fag.' Alva opened her handbag, produced cigarettes, lighted two, then handed one to Helen.

Helen tried a smile for size.

'Careful,' warned Alva. 'You might stop feeling sorry for yourself.'

The smile broadened and Helen said, 'I'm worried.'

'They'll pull it off,' soothed Alva.

'I only hope . . .'

'Don't hope. *Know.*' Alva drew on her cigarette. 'My David can sandpaper elephants down to greyhounds. And your old man's no slouch.'

'If we could only help.'

'We can help by being their womenfolk. That's all they

ask. What they *don't* want is a couple of miserable bitches waiting to tell them how they did it all wrong.'

'I'm – I'm sorry.'

'Yeah, you keep saying that. Now for a change stop being sorry. Start being lively. It comes easy with practice.'

'You're a heartless woman, Alva Hoyle.'

'Aren't I just?'

But the exchange was accompanied by mutual grins, and Alva knew she'd won through.

'What do we talk about?' she asked. 'And *not* bobbying.'

'Tell me about Wales,' suggested Helen. 'I've never been there.'

'Wales.' A slightly dreamy expression took over Alva's eyes. Her voice took on a mild, nostalgic lilt. 'Choirs and coal mines, my love. They go together. It gets some of the old dust from the tubes, see. Those male voice choirs. The chapels and the valleys. I'll tell you this, love. There's nobody better than a good Welshman . . . and nobody worse than a bad one.

'You know something? The Black Mountains. South Wales. Round Powys and Dyfed way. King Arthur country, see? Never mind what the old Cornish people say. The Black Mountains. They do say the Holy Chalice is hidden there somewhere. That's how the legend goes. Hidden away in the Black Mountains. Just a handful of people know where, and they won't tell. *Daren't* tell. Down from father to son, see? A direct line from Arthur himself. Makes you think. Makes you wonder . . .'

She had the Welsh gift of the tongue, and she was talking of the place she loved. Right or wrong – fact or fantasy – it mattered not at all. It was delightful to listen to, and Helen listened and became happy.

'. . . this "innocent man".' Hoyle paused to light another cigarette, then continued, 'We're talking about you, of course. What chance you have with a Not Guilty plea. No

132

exaggeration, Wardman. At this moment you don't think so, but while you're in prison you'll realise the truth. That I'm trying to help you. Promising you nothing, of course. No deals. We can't do that. But, let's say *we* didn't like Richardson. We didn't send a wreath. But he was murdered. You murdered him. Therefore I'm trying to help. Being objective. Making *you* be objective. Showing what you're up against, and how hopeless it is.

'We have to tell the truth in court. As simple as that. No varnish. No "verbals". Just what you've done. What you've said.

'Take your own admission. You were in Lessford at the time of the murder. You needn't have *been* in Lessford. You *should* have been in Bordfield, but instead you were in Lessford. Visiting Richardson. Two gays. An excuse, perhaps. But a very weak excuse when placed alongside everything else you've told us. Even weaker – indeed it becomes no excuse at all – when we know what *we* know. That you're a man with a temper. A violent man. We can't give that in evidence, but we don't need to. We've enough without that. Previous convictions have a bearing on the sentence, Wardman. The judge will be told and *he* decides whether or not to add a rider to the sentence. A violent man who, when caught and convicted, hasn't even *tried* to assist the police. He'll stiffen you, Wardman. He'll put you away for ever. And why? Because you're a damn fool. Because you won't even help yourself. Because we can't say anything – *anything*! – in your favour . . .'

The A1(M), the traffic roundabout and now the A1 proper. Thank Christ for small mercies! Despite the flash of oncoming headlights, undipped by idiots who shouldn't be allowed behind a wheel . . . thank Christ for small mercies. Home ground. A few more miles. A nothing to the distance they'd travelled that day. Then home. A hot bath; a long soak in steaming, sudded water. Just a few more miles.

133

The motor patrol sergeant hung onto that promise like a drowning man clinging to a spar. Not the driving. The driving was second nature. No sweat. Driving was dead easy. But that bloody, never-ending monologue from the rear seat . . . Jesus!

He'd always thought Hoyle to be a nice guy. Quiet, good at his job, but inoffensive. No way! He could be – he *was* – a bastard. A lousy, ruthless, sadistic bastard.

Wardman?

Wardman was taking stick. All the stick in the universe. And that wasn't right. The hell it was right. Richardson had been one of those people born to be murdered, hated even by his own kind. A louse who could have been stamped upon years ago. Who *should* have been stamped upon years ago. He (the motor patrol sergeant) could name a dozen people who might have been capable of killing him. Who *would* have killed him, given half a chance of getting away with it. So, why give Wardman such a rough time? Why skin the poor slob alive? Why, why, why?

It was wrong. It was all wrong. It couldn't possibly be right.

'. . . You say Richardson was alive when you left. That's your story, Wardman. Your *first* story. You called, but he was alive when you left. A lie. A little pressure – not much – and you change the yarn. He wasn't alive when you left. He wasn't even alive when you *arrived*. That is what we are now expected to believe. What the jury is expected to believe. Alive in one version. Dead in another. Lie after lie after lie.

'Embellish it a little. The way you've embellished it since we started this drive. Your friend. Richardson, your friend. Your fellow-homosexual. You visit him at Lessford. Buddies. But he didn't ask you to stay the night. Just "Hello" and "Goodbye". Friends! That's not how friends behave, Wardman. Not at all how friends behave. These things you've said. These variations *we'll* have to say in the witness box. Think about them. Think how much you'd believe anybody who switched yarns as often as that. The variations. Remember? You didn't use the bathroom, you *did* use the bathroom. You didn't stay, you stayed to talk. He let you in, you have your own key. Wardman, to put it mildly – very mildly indeed – you haven't a leg to stand on . . .'

Jean Belamy sat in nightie and dressing-gown, with her bare feet tucked under her and, in the comfort of an armchair, contemplated the life she'd unknowingly let herself in for. A good life? Oh, yes, at first. While Dick had been a mere copper – what he now contemptuously called a 'wooden-top' – those had been happy days. A great man in those days. To her a god among men. Rough diamond, but gentle.

Virility. A sad – almost nostalgic – smile brushed her lips as the word caught on her musings, like a length of thread caught on the material of a skirt. Virility. He'd been so proud. 'When I stop wanting to make love to you, you'll have something to worry about.' Not that he was over-sexed. Nothing like that. Nor, come to that, was she under-sexed, at least she didn't think so. Certainly not frigid. Just joyful, happy love-making. Spiced with animal passion occasionally. Enough to make it something more than cold-blooded copulation. The real thing and often, but not any more.

Okay, they were getting older. Not old, but older. But these days . . .

She almost chuckled to herself. A sad, slightly bitter chuckle.

Women were supposed to have 'headaches'. It was the woman who 'didn't feel like it'. It was *they* who felt 'too tired'.

But not in *this* house. Not in *this* family.

The job, of course. Eight-hour shifts were a thing of the long past. These days he worked to the point of exhaustion. Almost every day, too. Often all night. *Very* often into the small hours.

Bobbies! Coppers, jacks, wooden-tops, squad men. They spoke a language of their own. A language she only half-understood. But few people gave thought to the *wives* of these coppers, these jacks, these wooden-tops, these squad men. One day somebody would . . . somebody *might*. Some statistician. My God, he was in for a shock. The broken-marriage rate. The number of women – the number of wives – who said 'Enough!'. Who walked away from a man they'd once loved, because the damn job was far more demanding than any mistress. Something you couldn't fight. Something which, at best, you accepted with as much grace as possible, but secretly hated.

'. . . so time's running out, Wardman. Fast. Once we reach Lessford – once we note all you've said, all the twists and turns you've made, in our notebooks and from there on the file – that's it, my friend. That is the end, as far as you're concerned. God knows, you've been given enough time. More time than most men in your position. Time to think things out. Christ, you've had all the time in the world. Think man, *think*! Your fingerprints on the shower curtain. The blood group – Richardson's blood group – on every dab. In the shower trap. And you started off by spinning some damn fool yarn about showering because you were "grimy". About Richardson still being *alive*. About the two of you sitting around in the nude, talking. Which blasted lie do you expect a jury to believe? Or do you seriously think they'll believe *anything*?'

Wardman?

Oh yes, even Wardman knew he had to crack. He was holding it back for the right moment. No more than that.

Belamy had done his bit. The hard-neck routine; the routine he'd expected; the routine he'd been part of before and which he scorned. To crack for Belamy would have been wrong. Weak. Stupid. It would have made Belamy seem the sort of man he certainy was not.

But Hoyle. Hoyle represented the irresistible force. The slow pressure towards the edge which was impossible to contain. The argument without a counter-argument – that was Hoyle.

Therefore he (Wardman) was going to crack. He *had* to crack.

The only question was . . . when?

'. . . that slightly ridiculous escape attempt. Innocent men don't make a run for it, Wardman. They don't climb from one toilet to another, then worm their way through a window. Not *innocent* men. Not even frightened men.

'You're not a fool. Not a complete fool. Surely to God you can put yourself in the shoes of some jury member, listen to the garbage you've told us on this ride, and then . . .'

'I'm pulling in here.'

The monologue was interrupted. The motor patrol sergeant spoke in a louder than normal voice. Almost a shout. He swung the Cortina into a narrow side-road, braked at a gap in the hedge then dived from the driving seat. Leaving the door of the car open, he folded forward and was physically sick.

The others watched, saw him gradually straighten, take some deep breaths, wipe his lips with a handkerchief then return to the car with a slow and slightly unsteady walk.

'Better?' asked Belamy, as the motor patrol sergeant eased himself behind the wheel again.

The motor patrol sergeant nodded, closed the door, clipped the seat-belt into position, then drove the car slowly forward, looking for a place to turn.

'Something you've eaten?' suggested Belamy.

137

The motor patrol sergeant nodded a second time, but still didn't speak.

Nor was it 'something he'd eaten'. It was the build-up. The increasing tension. Like stage fright, but a thousand times worse than stage fright. He'd thought he'd seen everything. Experienced everything. Road accidents, blood and carnage all over the place, hysteria . . . the lot. But nothing like this. This was like being present in some torture chamber, with the rack being notched up and up every second. No screams – no *audible* screams – but the screams were there. They were part of the atmosphere. A silent accompaniment to Hoyle's constant, never-ending talk.

Wardman. What the hell must Wardman be feeling like? Twisting, turning, doubling back on himself. Innocence – even *possible* innocence – wasn't part of this game. But, great God, he *was* innocent! Hoyle went great guns about juries and what verdict a jury might reach. But Wardman was *innocent*. Among other things the law said so. Go no farther than the Presumption of Innocence . . . *Wardman was innocent*. And they (the police) represented the law. Decency. Fair play.

Or should . . .

The motor patrol sergeant eased the car into the mouth of a bridle-path, stopped, reversed and with consummate ease executed a perfect three-point-turn, then headed back towards the main road.

'. . . you drove home, you drove south on the A1. This road – but not the motorway – all the way to London and beyond. To the south coast. The weapon? Who knows? Who cares? Somewhere alongside the A1 at a guess. It won't be found, but that's not important. We don't *need* the weapon. We have too many other things. The expense of the search couldn't be justified. Not with what we already have. Not with your own nest of lies.

138

'Wardman, you may not believe me – I don't give a damn whether or not you believe me – but the truth is you're trussed tighter than any Christmas turkey. We'll call witnesses, but they won't *really* be needed. What you've already said. A great wall of untruths. Too high, too solid, too wide. You've built it. You! Nobody has put words into your mouth. Nobody has even *suggested* things. All yours, Wardman. Every sentence. Every word. You're a murderer, convicted out of your own mouth, and you haven't the sense to see it . . .'

Clarke knew why the patrol sergeant had brought his heart up. Too true, he knew. Clarke, too, was a spectator in the torture chamber; he, too, was witnessing a man being systematically torn limb from limb; he, too, felt sickened by it.

More than that even.

The steel links which attached him to Wardman seemed to carry some of the shock being received by the prisoner. Some of the silent anguish. Some of the hopelessness.

That and the tiredness.

God, he was tired! The tiredness numbed the senses, otherwise he, too, might have spewed his ring up alongside the motor patrol sergeant. Being a copper, eh? Being holier-than-thou. But they weren't, see? Belamy was a bastard. If anything, Hoyle was an even bigger bastard. Surprise, surprise! But it shouldn't have been. The rank was the thing. The higher the rank, the bigger the bastard. At least as far as C.I.D. was concerned. He hadn't realised it before. But *obviously*. Rungs of the ladder, see? The bloody ladder didn't go up – only the rank went up – the rungs of the ladder went *down*.

God, he was tired!

Mind you, Wardman was as mad as an escapee from a nut-house. Tell a yarn, then stick to it. Okay, they can prove it's cobblers. Let them prove it's cobblers. *Make* them prove it's cobblers. Don't switch and change like a drunken lunatic. Don't do their damn work *for* them. And, for Christ's sake, don't make a run for it. That really puts you in the schnook. Jesus! He *deserved* to be put away.

'. . . and inside. I don't have to tell *you*, Wardman. You've been there. You *know* what it's like. You'll find so-called "lovers". That I don't have to tell you. But there's another side. *You killed one of their kind.* Don't forget that. The longer you're in, the more dangerous it will become. One of them will shiv you . . . eventually. Sooner or later. Maybe one of Richardson's pals. A long term. They'll get you, Wardman. As sure as night follows day, they'll get you. Given long enough . . .'

'It makes David very special.' Alva Hoyle's eyes shone as she spoke. 'I mean, he isn't even a *Welshman*. Yorkshire. A stupid county, really. They think more about cricket than rugby. I tell you, my dad almost disowned me when I told him I was going to marry a Yorkshireman.'

'And not even a pitman,' smiled Helen.

'No, indeed.' Alva matched smile for smile. 'But Dad likes him now. Loves him, in fact. Even Yorkshire. He came up a few years back and we took him into the Dales. "Almost as good as Wales," he said. That was a great moment, I can tell you.'

'He's a fine man.' Helen still smiled.

'Dad?'

'David.'

'Oh . . . David.' She tilted her head and gave the impression of studying a point in space, slightly above eye-level and at less than a yard distant. 'He is a – how can I put it? There's a very fancy word for it – autodidact. A *would-be* autodidact. And that, my love, makes him a pain.'

'What on earth's an . . .'

'Autodidact? A bloke – anybody – self-taught to the point

140

where he's accepted as a scholar *by* scholars. They're around and, when they're genuine, they're great people. Enthusiasm instead of degrees, see? They've taken a subject – any subject, maybe more than one subject – learned it from top to bottom and side to side, then reduced it to ordinary language. They're kinky, in the nicest possible way.'

'And you don't like David being – er – kinky?'

'My pet.' Alva released an exaggerated sigh. 'David hasn't the time. He hasn't the concentration. And, in all honesty, he hasn't the old grey matter. He's a copper – a damn good copper – but that's *all* he is. Plastering that with unnecessary top-dressing drives him – and me! – nuts.'

'You're not – er – I mean . . .' Helen frowned.

'Oh, my love, I wouldn't change him.' Alva laughed aloud. 'I wouldn't leave him. He's my hubby. My man.'

'I'm glad.' Helen hesitated, then added, 'Because you *are* a scholar, my dear. No false modesty. Your brain . . .'

'My brain,' interrupted Alva grimly, 'is a bigger bloody nuisance than that thing *you* have wrapped around you. And as obvious.'

'I don't see . . .'

'David,' said Alva, 'is a male chauvinist pig. All Yorkshiremen are. The Greer woman wouldn't have lasted five minutes north of the Wash. The bread-winner, the boss. Very simple. Very basic. Very *nice*, if you have the right sort of man . . . and that's my David. Very secure. But they want to be best – to *feel* best – in everything. David wants that, but can't get it. He'll never get it, and there's not a thing I can do to convince him. My God! Do you know what we have to listen to? Have to watch on the box? Open University. We listen to and watch crap that's no use to either of us. Because *he* wants to know. Everything about everything.' She blew out her cheeks. 'Who the hell cares about craft design and technology? About archaeology as a background to ancient history? About the oldest out-

141

cropping rocks in the U.K.? Who the hell *cares*? It's grasshopper knowledge, but he won't see that. He wants to be able to talk about these things. That's his excuse. What he can't see is that *his* job, and the way he does it, beats all those cockeyed subjects into a – a . . .'

'Cocked hat?' supplied Helen.

Alva sighed, and said, 'Oh, for one more chance to watch *Casablanca*. Even *Gone With the Wind*.'

'. . . you go into the witness box. If you *don't* go into the witness box, what you say will count for nothing. If you *do* go into the witness box, you'll be cross-examined. Think about that, Wardman. Cross-examined by a Q.C. and torn to pieces. He'll . . .'

'*All right*!' Wardman almost shouted the interruption, then, in a quieter tone, he repeated, 'All right.'

It seemed that the timing was perfect. Almost deliberate. The exclamation coincided with the Cortina slowing down slightly and leaving the A1 for the roads leading to Lessford.

Hoyle waited.

Wardman muttered, 'I haven't a leg to stand on.'

'You're licked,' agreed Hoyle quietly.

Belamy raised his chin from his chest. Lack of sleep and the long journey had almost forced his eyes to close. Now he was wide awake, and listening.

In a steady, controlled voice, Wardman said, 'You want me to say I murdered Richardson.'

'I want you to tell the truth.'

'But . . . that I murdered Richardson?'

'The truth,' repeated Hoyle.

Wardman's body was not as steady as his voice. Clarke could feel the slight tremble as the prisoner fought to retain control. It was an effort. A physical effort. The muscles of his right arm quivered, like a bow-string after the release of an arrow.

142

'If – if I say I killed him . . .'

'No deals,' cut in Hoyle.

'I mean . . .'

'This isn't a bargaining counter, Wardman. We don't *need* a confession.'

'But – but if I did?'

'You'd be doing yourself some good. That's advice, not a deal.'

The motor patrol sergeant concentrated upon driving. Every nerve. Every muscle. He tried not to listen, but that was impossible. Behind him, a man had been reduced to dust. Dust without dignity. Dust . . . ready to be blown away.

Wardman said, 'I don't know where the weapon is.'

'That's not important.'

'If – if I killed him, I used a weapon.'

'*If* you killed him?'

There was a silence, then Wardman said, 'What I told you before.'

'What about it?'

'Evidence?'

'We'll go easy,' promised Hoyle, then added, 'If you'll let us.'

'If – er – if I make a statement?' suggested Wardman.

'That's up to you.'

'Saying I killed him?'

Hoyle moved his shoulders.

Wardman muttered, 'The truth is, I didn't like him too much.'

'I wouldn't know,' said Hoyle flatly.

'Just that, if I'd had anywhere else . . . To go, I mean.'

Hoyle waited.

Wardman said, 'Let me think about it.'

'Think about it?' Hoyle pretended surprise.

'What, y'know, what I'm going to do next.'

'It's already arranged.' Hoyle's voice was low and grim.

'You're going to stand in a Crown Court dock charged with the murder of Clive Richardson . . . and from there you're going to a prison cell.'

Flensing worried. Flensing had something to worry about. This little lot was a gamble; by far the biggest gamble of his police career. If it came off there'd be a rose garden, maybe. But if it *didn't* come off!

Nor were the cards too near the chest any more. Screwing up evidence was frowned upon, and *those* cards had already been dealt. Must have been by this time. Wardman was no mug. No grass-green cowboy. Wardman knew police tactics, what he didn't know was *Flensing's* tactics.

Therefore, a gamble.

He lighted a cigarette and prowled his office, and his thoughts turned sour because of the worry. Sour and bitter and, perhaps, not a little self-pitying.

Helen edged her way into his thinking. The truth was, Helen was never far from his thoughts. Helen . . . a wife who couldn't *be* a wife . . . in effect, and as far as he was concerned, a head with no body. He was a louse for seeing things that way, but what other way? He was also a fully paid-up member of the male section of the human race. He had feelings. He had urges. He was no saint, and celibacy hadn't been part of his marriage vows. So, he was a louse?

Dammit, why was he thinking these thoughts? He had more important things to worry about.

More important things?

Did it matter? Did it *really* matter whether Wardman played things the way he and Hoyle had arranged that he should play things? Did it really *matter*? Damnation, all his life he (Flensing) had had his arm above the elbow in some blasted cesspit or another. If it wasn't Richardson, it was some other crawling bastard who shouldn't have been born. Some thieving hound. Some foul specimen of

144

humanity. Therefore, whether or not Wardman 'coughed' on his way north wasn't *so* important. He coughed, he didn't cough. It worked or it didn't work. Who the hell cared? Today, tomorrow, this year, next year some *real* criminal was going to press a button, and after that there'd be damn all left to care about.

Policing? Murder? Iron lungs? Celibacy?

The whole shooting match. It all boiled down to keeping things on the simmer until some trigger-happy bastard turned the gas too high.

The cats' eyes caught the beams from the headlights and raced towards them. Tiny orbs of temporary brilliance guiding the motor patrol sergeant round the bends and twists of the road. And his tiredness was such that they seemed to hit his eyes like a never-ending stream of miniature explosions.

He was a good driver – a police-trained driver – and he knew he should stop. Stretch a little. Take a walk away from, then back to, the car. Breathe clean, night air. Forget driving, if only for a few minutes.

Not possible!

Headquarters was too near. The damn car smelled like a wrestler's armpit, what with stale cigarette smoke, and what else. The road noise was like a tiny electric drill pushing holes in his skull. His facial muscles ached from a jaw he seemed unable to unclench.

Damnation, he should stop, but not possible.

Wardman said, 'A statement.'

'What about a statement?' Hoyle's question was flat and emotionless.

'You like statements. You people ... you *like* statements.'

'Not when they're unnecessary.'

'I've ...' Wardman took a deep breath. 'I've given it some thought.'

145

'You were going to.'

'Proof. Y'know, circumstantial evidence.'

'A damn sight more than "circumstantial".'

'All right, the evidence.' Wardman moved his head. 'That file.'

'Enough. We don't need a statement.'

'To give my side, I mean.' The hint of desperation touched Wardman's tone.

'*Your* side?'

'Everything's against me. Everything!'

'What the hell else? You killed a man.'

'I . . .' Wardman stopped, swallowed, then said, 'But *my* side of things. Possible reasons. I'm allowed that, surely?'

'Excuses?'

'Reasons, if you like. Good God, I'm allowed to give *my* side of things.'

'Explanations?'

'They're there.' Wardman shook his head, then whispered, 'I'm allowed to say *something*.'

'That you tried to escape from police custody?'

'I was scared. I can explain that.'

'That you've changed your tale about six times?'

'That, too. Reasons.'

'You're as guilty as hell, Wardman. What excuses?'

'Reasons.'

'For Christ's sake!' Belamy could remain silent no longer. He half turned in the front passenger seat and growled, 'If the louse wants to make a statement, why not?'

'Do you want to make a statement, Wardman?' asked Hoyle.

'I – I think so.'

'Only "think"?'

'Yes . . . I'd like to make a statement.'

'It's not necessary.'

'Please!'

'What good would it do? What good do you think it

146

would do?'

'Inspector . . .'

'Shut up, sergeant.' Then to Wardman. 'Come on. What good do you think it would do?'

Wardman moistened his lips, seemed to pause long enough to gather wits and words, then spoke in a low, intense but broken-hearted tone.

'You. Inspector Hoyle. I – I think you're a good man. A very honest man. The job's bad. Policing . . . that's bad. But you do it as humanely as possible . . .'

'Get on with it, Wardman.'

'What you say. I believe you. I don't think you'd lie. The evidence is there in that file . . . and the evidence says I killed Clive Richardson. Murdered him. No hope . . . that's what I'm getting at. The more I scream "I didn't", the worse I make things for myself. I'm – I'm prepared to believe that. Your advice. I'm prepared to take it.

'Cross-examination. As you say – the lies I've already told, the fact that I tried to make a run for it – I'd be cut to ribbons. I don't want that. Anything but that. Plead Guilty, see? Don't waste the time of the court. Don't upset the judge. Do all I can to please everybody. It might – it just *might* – knock a few years off the sentence. I don't know, but it's worth a try.'

He paused for a moment, then continued, 'But I'd like my side – y'know, *my* side – heard in court. Not told by a lawyer, see? Told by me. No fancy "pleading". I don't think that would help. I believe you, it wouldn't help. He couldn't say anything. But *my* words. The way I tell it. That – that Richardson was rotten. That the only thing we had in common was . . .'

Again, a pause and a moistening of the lips.

He went on, 'I'm not a talker. That's all. In court, with all the wigs and gowns – with the judge up there – I'd dry up. I wouldn't be able. But if I made a statement. Y'know, a *statement*. That's all you'd need. A Guilty plea, no

147

evidence, then read my statement. What *I* have to say. What I couldn't put into words. Read out for me by you. By one of your men. I'm – I'm entitled to that, aren't I?'

'You're entitled to that,' agreed Hoyle.

'That's what I want then. When we reach Bordfield. Just write it down for me . . . one of you. Put down what I say. Everything I say. As I say it. I'll plead Guilty. Lower court, Crown Court . . . all along the line. No conditions. Just Guilty, then read my statement. What I'd like to say, but what I know I won't be able to say. Then if – look, I'm not making conditions, but if you will, please – soft pedal all I've said since you picked me up. When I tried to run for it, that sort of thing. I want . . .'

He stopped talking. He was a beaten man with his back to a wall. It was there in his voice. In the droop of his shoulders. In the great atmosphere of defeat and heartbreak which seemed to fill the speeding Cortina.

'What?' asked Hoyle, gently.

'I – I don't want to spend the rest of my life in prison,' he whispered. 'That's all. Let me do *something* – *say* something – to convince the judge. Never again, see? You – you have me.'

'Pinned to the floor with six-inch nails,' agreed Hoyle.

He nodded, then breathed, 'Just give me the chance to beg for *some* freedom . . . eventually.'

EIGHT

The night shift patrol men hadn't yet come in for supper. Another hour – thereabouts – and they'd be drifting in, unpacking their sandwiches and wandering over to the hot drinks machine. Tea, coffee, cocoa, soup. Maybe even soft drinks after the heat of the day. Some damn fool would switch on the radio and lunatic D.J. talk would alternate between noise masquerading as music. There would never be many men in the canteen at any one moment; they'd come in in small groups, then be replaced as they returned to the streets over a period of more than two hours. But for the moment, apart from the motor patrol sergeant and the night-duty C.I.D. stand-by, D.C. Shaw, the room was empty. Empty and grubby. The cleaners would arrive at a little after six, the ash-trays would be emptied, the table-tops wiped down and polished, the floor swept and every-thing would be tidied up and put in its proper place, but for now . . .

The motor patrol sergeant sipped tea from a plastic beaker, drew on a cigarette and figured the canteen reflec-ted his own feelings. Very tired, not a little disorientated and, above all else, sullied.

His intention had been to park the Cortina, collect his own car, then go home for a bath and bed.

Hoyle had said, 'Hang around, sergeant. You may be required.'

'But, sir, I . . .'

'Just hang around. I'll let you know. Be in the canteen, then I'll know where to contact you.'

'You look shattered, sergeant,' observed Shaw with a smile.

'Shattered?' The motor patrol sergeant repeated the word slowly. He nodded, then mused, 'Y'know, son, that's just about the right word. Shattered. Shell-shocked. Bomb-happy.'

'A hell of a long journey. There and back in the day.'

'Not just the journey.'

'No?' Shaw looked puzzled.

'A long way . . . true.' The motor patrol sergeant sipped at the tea. 'But other things. Far worse things.'

'The accident? I hear you . . .'

'No. Not the accident . . . although that didn't help.'

'In that case . . .'

'I would not,' said the motor patrol sergeant heavily, 'have your job for a hundred quid an hour.'

Shaw's lips moved into a slow smile. C.I.D. was (he knew) a very demanding department of law-enforcement. It was nice to be appreciated. The smile turned into a scowl, as the motor patrol sergeant continued his little speech.

'To work for – to take orders from – bastards like Belamy and Hoyle. Not if I needed a wheelbarrow to take home the wage.'

'Hey! Wait a minute . . .'

'Belamy I knew about. Had heard about. Okay, he's worse than rumour has it, but not much worse. Hoyle on the other hand. Brother!'

'What's wrong with Hoyle?' Shaw's eyes hardened.

'Today has been a watershed in my life, son.' The motor patrol sergeant drew on the cigarette and stared at the canteen wall beyond and above Shaw's shoulder. He seemed to be talking to himself. Quietly. Solemnly. As if reminding himself of things he'd previously counted as too

150

outrageous to contemplate. 'I've heard the chestnut about it taking a bastard to nail a bastard. Lots and lots of times, I've heard that one. I've never believed it until today. Now, I'll never *dis*believe it.'

'Look, if you're suggesting . . .'

'Son, you weren't there.' The motor patrol sergeant met Shaw's angry gaze, eye-to-eye. 'You were not there. You didn't *hear* it. Wardman. I don't give a damn what Wardman is, what Wardman's done, no man deserves the sweet hell *he's* been wound through.'

'Questioned, you mean?'

'Questioned? Yeah – I suppose so – questioned, by Belamy. That was bad enough. But Hoyle didn't question him. Hoyle just talked . . . and talked . . . and talked. He didn't want answers. No way did that chief inspector of yours want answers. He didn't even leave gaps for answers. He was gloating, son. Gloating! That poor bleeder Wardman was systematically *tortured*. Nothing less. Mentally and psychologically tortured . . . and Hoyle couldn't stop. That's how much the bastard enjoyed himself. Talk about sadism. He bloody well *enjoyed* it.'

'You're talking about Detective Chief Inspector Hoyle,' warned Shaw coldly.

'That's who I'm talking about,' agreed the motor patrol sergeant.

'I'll not sit here and listen to a fine man . . .'

'A *what*?'

'Dammit, he's worth ten . . .'

'Don't get uppity, son.' The motor patrol sergeant had already had a gutful. Unaccustomed bite entered his tone as he snapped, 'This "fine man" you seem so anxious to defend. I've been with him all day. I've seen him in action at close quarters, and I don't like what I've seen. I've expressed an opinion. *My* opinion. But don't get stroppy, lad, just because I've expressed that opinion. Go tell him if you like. Go screw yourself for all I care. What you must

151

not do is think I'm going to sit here and take slaver from a pipsqueak like you. You may think, because you're C.I.D., that you're the cream from the top of the milk, but I out-rank you . . . by one rung. That means I can fizz you – *will* fizz you – if that mouth of yours runs away with itself. And that, my little C.I.D. hopeful, would just about make my day.'

Hoyle had said, 'Right. Into Number One Interview Room with him, Clarke.' Then to Belamy, 'He's all yours now, sergeant. He wants to make a statement. Make sure it's a good one.'

And Belamy had grinned, stretched luxuriously, having climbed from the car and answered, 'Sir, it will be some statement. Watertight, fireproof, the lot.'

'That's all I ask. Use Clarke as witness.'

'He's not like that,' argued Shaw.

The flash-point had passed. Shaw, despite his lack of years, was a sensible enough guy. He knew – he could see with his own eyes – that the motor patrol sergeant had had one hell of a day. Nor was the motor patrol sergeant one of those fizz-crazy types. That was all so much crap . . . to be accepted and dismissed as such.

As for the motor patrol sergeant. The spat of anger had passed; spurted and died like a badly-made firework. The tired and twisted grin gave full proof of that. They were both, therefore, back to as near "normal" as the o'clock, plus soul-weariness, would allow.

The motor patrol sergeant said, 'I've witnessed him at full-throttle, old son. Maybe you haven't.'

'I've worked with him a few times.'

The motor patrol sergeant grunted.

'He's always seemed decent. Fair-minded.'

'That's what I always thought.' The motor patrol sergeant moved a shoulder. 'He's not.'

'I can understand Belamy . . .'

'Belamy's a pig. One of the reasons we're all called pigs.'

'That's what I mean. But Hoyle?'

'Today . . .' The motor patrol sergeant stifled a yawn. 'Hoyle could have reached the winning post before Belamy moved into second gear.'

Hoyle flopped into the armchair in Flensing's office and sighed, 'Maybe.'

'Only "maybe"?' Flensing frowned.

'Christ, I've worked,' breathed Hoyle.

'A stiff drink?' Flensing strolled towards the booze-cupboard.

'That would be very nice.'

'Then we'll ring your wife. She's with Helen.'

'Not like Hoyle.'

Shaw's tone was that of a child suddenly faced with the horrible knowledge that Santa Claus had, for all these years, been a con trick.

'Nobody reaches that rank without rough edges,' soothed the motor patrol sergeant. 'It happens. I've seen it too many times.'

'But *Hoyle*,' pleaded Shaw.

'All right, he's your pin-up boy.' The motor patrol sergeant waved a tired hand. 'Live with your dreams, son. Be happy.'

Belamy had closed the door of Number One Interview Room, then waved a hand towards a chair.

He'd said, 'Right, you horrible creature, sit down. Pull a chair up to the table and make yourself comfortable. We're here for a long time.'

He'd turned to Clarke.

'Unlock the cuffs, constable, then you find a chair . . . and after that, *nothing*. You're here to listen, and that's the only reason you're here.'

Belamy had positioned a third chair at the table, opened a drawer and taken out a batch of statement forms. As Clarke had unlocked the handcuffs, and the two other occupants had seated themselves, Belamy had continued speaking.

'A statement. You want to make a statement. Great. You tell me, I'll write it down. Don't be coy, sonny. Don't be shy. You won't shock anybody. All the gory, filthy details, right? But first of all *I* have to put down a few things. Name, address, occupation . . . that sort of guff. Then the usual garbage about nobody tearing an arm off and beating you over the head with it to make you talk. In polite language, of course. But that's what it boils down to. Then you sign, *then* you talk. You tell it all. Understand? Because if you don't tell it all it's not worth a damn, and all the other ducking and weaving will have to be trotted out in court. So . . . *the lot*. Anything less and I'm not interested . . .'

Helen turned her head as Alva opened the door and entered the ward.

'They're back,' smiled Alva.

'And?'

'Now it all depends on Belamy.' Alva closed the door and walked towards the bed and apparatus in the middle of the room.

'Oh, God!' murmured Helen.

'We knew it would, my pet,' soothed Alva. 'Anything else would have been a miracle.'

Helen straightened her head and stared disconsolately at the ceiling.

'We knew it, my pet,' repeated Alva. 'Belamy is part *of* it.'

'Such a foul person,' whispered Helen.

'Let's keep our fingers crossed and hope foul enough.'

'We'll start off by taking the bull by the horns.' Belamy's ballpoint was poised above the statement forms. 'How about, "I am a sexual deviant and often call at the home of Clive Richardson in order to practise my perversions"? A nice juicy start to the statement.'

'That's not quite true,' muttered Wardman.

'No?' Belamy frowned, then his expression cleared, and he said, 'No, of course not. Wrong tense. "I often *called* at . . ." Not much point in calling now.'

'I – er – I don't like the word "often".'

'Don't let's *start* by splitting hairs, sonny. You went when you could, right?'

'I suppose so.'

'Which was as often as possible?'

'Ye-es.'

'Fine.' Belamy began to write. '"I am a sexual deviant and, as often as possible, called at the home of Clive Richardson." Let's get that established for a start.'

'If Belamy lays it on too thick . . .' mused Hoyle.

'Belamy will be Belamy,' drawled Flensing. 'He'll do what he thinks should be done . . . his way.'

'His way,' agreed Hoyle. He tasted the whisky. 'What pleasure does he get from it, I wonder?'

'Does he get pleasure?' countered Flensing.

'It doesn't seem to upset him.'

'It's his job as he sees it. *He* doesn't think it's the wrong way.'

'He must be a fool,' said Hoyle bluntly.

'No, not a fool.' Flensing smiled. 'Not over-wise, of course. But not a fool. He deals in extremes. He doesn't understand – doesn't even acknowledge – grey areas.'

'By my yardstick, he's a fool,' insisted Hoyle. 'More than that, he's a dangerous fool.'

'All right, you're at Bordfield,' said Belamy. 'Let's put it

155

this way. "I was at Bordfield. I felt like having some sexual kicks, so I decided to visit Richardson in Lessford." That about it?'

Wardman nodded dumbly.

Belamy wrote the words on the statement form.

'There has to be a reason,' muttered Shaw.

The motor patrol sergeant grunted, left the table, refilled his beaker with fresh tea, then returned.

'That's not like Hoyle,' insisted Shaw. 'It's not the way he works.'

'I wouldn't know.' The motor patrol sergeant gave the impression of being too tired to care.

'I mean, there has to be a *reason*.'

'Look, son, I'm knackered.' The motor patrol sergeant sipped at his fresh drink and patted his pocket for cigarettes. 'Why in hell's name I'm here is beyond me. Hoyle told me to wait. I'm waiting. Why? That's *his* closely guarded secret. All I know for certain is that some bugger's going to cough up overtime. Hoyle isn't *my* pet policeman, so I obey orders because he carries the rank, but I don't do it out of the goodness of my heart.'

Belamy stared the length of the table at Wardman. He paused for thought before continuing the statement.

He said, 'Now we come to the fancy bits. You say you've a key for Richardson's place?'

Wardman nodded.

'So, you let yourself in, Richardson was there. He was in the nude, you stripped off, then you got down to it. That about sum it up?'

Again Wardman moved his head and sighed. He seemed to be in a dream; completely unaware and completely uninterested in his surroundings. Clarke watched him and felt like weeping. The man was empty; devoid of all feeling; a vacuum as far as any emotion was concerned. Policing –

156

even hard-line policing – didn't demand this. Nobody, not even a suspected murderer, deserved *this*.

Belamy was saying, 'Straightforward language, sonny. That's what we need. Let's say, "I have a key for Richardson's home. I use it when I wish to indulge in homosexual practices with him. I used it on this night and for that purpose".'

Wardman's eyes remained dead. He said nothing, and Belamy took the silence for agreement and continued writing the statement.

Then, 'The actual fun and games. How about, "Richardson was naked when I arrived. I stripped, and was also naked. We indulged ourselves, as was our normal practice on such occasions". That should fit the bill, don't you think?'

Hoyle glanced at his watch and murmured, 'Christ, they're taking their time.'

'Patience, David.'

Flensing's rank showed. The reason why he held the rank. Given time, Hoyle would learn. Patience, but more than that and more important than that. A quiet acceptance that all that *could* be done *had* been done. Thereafter, a calmness.

Flensing scooped up Hoyle's empty glass, returned to the booze-cupboard, splashed whisky into the empty glass and also into a second glass. He handed Hoyle his glass, then settled himself in the swivel-chair behind the desk.

'It's happening in Number One Interview Room,' he said quietly. '*What's* happening, we don't know. We can only guess . . . and hope we're right. At this moment we can't influence anything.'

'We need that statement.' Hoyle moistened his lips.

'Of course.' Flensing's lips moved into a slow, momentary smile. 'Belamy is very busy getting it for us. It's worth remembering.'

157

'Belamy!' breathed Hoyle.

'Quite.'

'What if he doesn't?'

'In that case,' said Flensing gently, 'we come unstuck. Today has been wasted. We – I in particular – have some very awkward questions to answer, and we have an undetected murder on the books. Not a nice prospect, I agree, but what else?'

'The end of your career. The end of mine. At the very least, the end of our respective reputations.'

'Possibly,' agreed Flensing calmly. 'Indeed *probably*. It's what we're paid for, David. To use an expression . . . it's why we joined.'

'For the sake of scum like Richardson.' Bitterness was in Hoyle's tone.

'No.' Flensing shook his head slowly. 'For the sake of *our* peace of mind. We can, at least, say we tried. We did our best to put a murderer in a Crown Court dock. It isn't important who he murdered. That he *committed* murder, that's enough.'

'The public won't see it that way. When the newspapers . . .'

'Either way, it will be news,' drawled Flensing. 'They'll report it, embellish it, probably mis-quote both of us and, if we aren't very careful, get our respective ranks and names wrong. You're too old a hand to worry about that, David.' Flensing paused, sipped whisky, then continued. 'The public? We owe the public nothing, David. No explanations. No apologies. Nothing. Oh, they *think* we do.' He waved a languid hand. 'But that's only because certain minorities make far too much noise. They divert attention. They concentrate interest upon the criminal rather than the crime . . . rather than the *victim*. Of course we're "wrong". We represent the Law, the Law represents restrictions and nobody likes being restricted. So *we're* "wrong". A man gets drunk – too drunk to look after himself – and we arrest him.

158

Don't expect him to thank us. A man drives like a maniac – endangers other members of the public – so we take steps to stop him from driving a car for a few years. He won't congratulate us. Small things . . . and big. Somebody commits murder. So, who can feel sorry for a corpse? That's what it boils down to. Sympathy has to go somewhere. The mugger, not the muggee . . . because the muggee shouldn't have been walking alone down a dark alley. The rapist, not the woman raped . . . she asked for it, she shouldn't have been walking alone in some isolated spot. Don't *worry* about it, David. Accept it. The world is inside out, back to front, upside down. You and me – people like us – we're crazy, therefore we're the only sane people around.'

'You're a cynic.' The grin was twisted and a little sad.

'Of course. Every conscientious police officer is a cynic . . . otherwise he'd be inside a padded cell within a month.'

'Did you have an argument?' asked Belamy. 'A row about something?'

Wardman didn't seem to hear.

'Answer me, sonny,' growled Belamy.

'I – I suppose so,' breathed Wardman.

'That's it, then. "We had an argument. A fight. We were both naked. That's why there was no blood on my clothes." That do?'

Without waiting for a reply, Belamy wrote the words onto the statement form.

He looked up and said, 'What was the row about? We'd better get that down.' He paused then, when Wardman made no answer, continued, 'Something to do with what you were up to? That has to be the answer, hasn't it? What the hell else do you turds fight about?'

Wardman turned his head. Slowly. Almost painfully. His frown of utter incomprehension deepened and he made a slight movement of his head. It may have been a nod. It may have been anything.

'Right.' Belamy was satisfied. 'Let's say, "During our sexual activities we had an argument. I lost my temper." How's that for a lead-in?'

Without waiting for a reply, Belamy started to write again.

Clarke made as if to speak, then changed his mind and closed his mouth.

'What I can never understand . . .'

Hoyle slowly realised that Flensing was talking for the sake of talking. To keep his mind – to keep both of their minds – occupied, rather than allowing silence to give the liberty to contemplate what might be happening in Number One Interview Room.

'What I can never understand,' said Flensing, 'is where these writer chaps get the notion of Scotland Yard being the big nick as far as the United Kingdom is concerned. Ever been there, David?'

'No.' Hoyle forced himself to concentrate.

'A little like the Vatican . . . or the Kremlin. All the ideas, but none of the action. A very rarified atmosphere. Map Rooms, TV Rooms, Information Rooms, all the gadgetry in the world – and, of course, dozens of wall-to-wall-luxury offices – but not a working flatfoot in sight.'

'The new place?'

'Yes, of course. The old place by the Thames – the walls were starting to crumble, because of the pressure of paper from inside. This one has more solid walls. More space. Bags more room for paper. And gold braid. Lots and lots of gold braid. The commissioner, of course. Then deputy commissioners. Assistant deputy commissioners. Assistant commissioners. Deputy assistant commissioners. The permutations are mind-boggling. Mere chief constables come well down in the pecking order. In fact the whole place is a . . .'

'Ralph, please!' Hoyle smiled as he interrupted. 'Scotland Yard wouldn't *dare* do what we've done.'

'No. Of course not.' Flensing returned the worried smile. 'It takes northern cunning.'

'Something like that.'

'Or northern stupidity.'

'Let's say we don't like murderers walking around in our neck of the woods.'

'Shall we pray?' grinned Flensing. 'That's about all we have left. Divine intervention.'

'And Belamy, of course.'

'Shall we say, "I went berserk"?' asked Belamy. 'It's a nice word. It means losing your marbles, and . . .'

'I know the meaning of the word "berserk",' sighed Wardman.

'Good. We'll use it then. You're both starkers, right? The slap-and-tickle bit's gone sour. Reason not specified. No need to. Poofties are half-way round the twist, anyway.'

'Are they really?'

'Eh?'

'It doesn't matter.' Wardman's tone was flat and expressionless.

'I'm trying to help you, sonny.' Belamy glared.

Wardman moved a shoulder just one shoulder and very little.

'I'm doing my best for you,' insisted Belamy.

Wardman remained silent.

Belamy continued, 'All right, let's put it this way. "We argued, because Richardson wouldn't do what I wanted him to do. I lost my temper and went berserk. I started hitting him over the head." That cover it?'

'If you say so.' The voice was as empty, as expressionless as ever.

'It's your statement, sonny.'

Wardman's lips moved a little and he murmured, 'You're writing it, sergeant. I'll sign it.'

161

'Good enough.' Belamy nodded. 'That's what we'll put then.'

The motor patrol sergeant scowled, then said, 'There's no good reason for me being here. I've had a long day and a rough day. I want bed.'

'Who doesn't?' Shaw stretched, then covered his mouth with a hand to counter a yawn. 'This night reserve shift wastes time.'

'I drive cars. I understand cars.' Each man seemed to be holding a separate conversation, not listening to the other, but speaking his thoughts aloud. 'Give me four wheels and a good engine under a bonnet. That's all I ask . . .'

'. . . You sit around – here or the C.I.D. room – waiting for what? If it's big, the circus gets called out. If it's small, it doesn't get reported until tomorrow morning . . .'

'. . . A well-serviced engine. Keep the oil right, keep the tyre pressure right. *That* won't let you down . . .'

'. . . I mean, think about it. What's likely to happen this time of night? What's likely to be reported? Stolen cars? They go straight out to you people. *I* can't find 'em . . .'

'. . . Night driving. I rather like night driving, really. After a good day's kip, of course. Quiet. Keep away from the main roads. Wild life, caught in the headlights. I've seen foxes. I've seen badgers. I've seen just about everything . . .'

'. . . Take rape. Some woman rushes in here saying she's just been raped. What good am *I*. She isn't going to tell *me* anything worth a damn. I'm not even married. I don't even have a girl friend. I wouldn't know which questions to ask. How to ask them . . .'

In effect, they talked to themselves. That they were sitting at the same table, supposedly keeping each other company, meant nothing. Neither was listening to the other.

There was a reason, but it was a strange reason. A reason

162

neither could have explained.

Lessford Regional Headquarters was a large building. It had many rooms, many corridors, and was as solidly built as any building in the city. Yet it seemed to be vibrating. Silently and without movement, but vibrating nevertheless. As if somewhere inside its great bowels an impossible tension was building up and was about to explode. A "feeling" . . . a feeling which reached into every corner of every room. It seemed to impregnate the whole building. Something – something terrible – was going to happen.

The bell of the canteen telephone rang.

Shaw pushed back his chair and walked across the parquet floor to answer it.

When he returned he said, 'Flensing's office. They want us both up there.'

The motor patrol sergeant nodded and stood up from the table. He seemed to have been expecting the summons.

Flensing replaced the receiver and glanced across at Hoyle.

'You – er – get the feel,' he drawled gently. 'The sort of now-or-never impression.'

Hoyle nodded, without saying anything. He understood. He was a working copper, therefore he understood. Something nobody could teach. Something never to be explained in any textbook. The *timing*. It was either right or it was wrong, but the decision had to be made . . . right *or* wrong.

As if on cue, they each drained what little whisky was left in their glasses, and Flensing stood up from the desk and returned the glasses to the booze-cupboard. He closed the cupboard door quietly, slowly, then returned to his chair behind the desk.

They waited in silence. Such was the state of their nerves that they almost jumped when the knock came on the door.

Flensing cleared his throat and called, 'Come in.'

The door opened and Clarke walked into the office. He

163

left the door slightly ajar then walked, stiff-legged, to within a foot of the front edge of Flensing's desk. He ignored Hoyle – didn't seem to be aware of Hoyle's presence – then drew himself to attention and, despite the fact that both he and Flensing were in civilian clothes, snapped off a salute. He remained standing at attention, his eyes fixed to a point above Flensing's head.

'Well?' asked Flensing softly.

'I can't be part of that statement, sir.'

The voice was low but controlled. No passion. No outrage. Just a bald delivery of fact.

'Wardman's statement?' said Flensing.

'It's *not* Wardman's statement, sir.' Clarke did not lower his eyes.

'Expand on that remark a little, constable.'

'Wardman hasn't made a statement, sir. He's hardly said a word. It's *Belamy's* statement. What Belamy wants him to say, in Belamy's own words.'

'*Sergeant* Belamy,' Flensing reminded him gently.

'Sergeant Belamy, sir,' echoed Clarke politely.

'You realise the seriousness of this accusation, constable?'

'Yes, sir.'

'That a sergeant – a detective sergeant with no small experience – is, to use an expression, "fitting out" a suspect?'

'He's entitled to a fair crack of the whip, sir.'

'Wardman?'

'Yes, sir. And he's not getting it. He's being made to sign a confession he hasn't made.'

'*Made*?'

'He'll sign it, sir. Nothing surer.'

'Physical violence?'

'No, sir.'

'Threats of physical violence?'

'No, sir.'

164

'Promises? Deals?'

'No, sir. Nothing like that, sir.'

'Constable.' Flensing leaned back in the chair. His voice was still a soft drawl, but with that hint of steel which his rank carried. 'We're talking about two men. One of them a detective sergeant. The other a man suspected – strongly suspected – of committing murder.'

'Yes, sir.'

Shaw and the motor patrol sergeant pushed the door wider and entered the office. Hoyle motioned them to silence, then waved them to two high-backed chairs positioned near the walls of the office and behind Clarke. Clarke didn't seem to notice their arival.

As Flensing continued speaking, Hoyle leaned forward and pushed the office door closed.

Flensing said, 'You've been handcuffed to Wardman all day, right?'

'Yes, sir.'

'Presumably Sergeant Belamy questioned Wardman in the car.'

'Yes, sir.'

'Did you raise any objections?'

'No, sir.'

'Why not?'

'It was . . . different, sir.'

'Different?'

Clarke kept his eyes fixed on the point above Flensing's head, and said, 'He claimed he was innocent, sir.'

'That's no answer, constable.'

'He told lies, but that's all.'

'Lies?'

'He changed his story a few times, sir.'

'Which story did *you* believe?' asked Flensing gently.

'Sir?'

'Constable, you're here to make a serious complaint. A serious accusation. You're not a fool . . . I'll give you the benefit of that doubt. Therefore, you must have grounds for that accusation. On your own admission, Wardman is a liar. He changes his story to suit whatever line any questioning might take. All the evidence we have proves he murdered Richardson. As I understand things, he volunteered to make a full statement concerning . . .'

'No, sir,' interrupted Clarke.

'I beg your pardon?'

'He didn't *volunteer*, sir. He was conned into it. Talked – frightened – into it.'

Flensing raised a sardonic eyebrow and murmured, 'Sergeant Belamy seems to be something of a . . .'

'Not Sergeant Belamy, sir.' Clarke moistened his lips and, for the first time lowered his eyes and looked directly into Flensing's face. He repeated, 'Not Sergeant Belamy.'

'No?' Flensing waited.

Clarke glanced sideways, then almost whispered, 'Chief Inspector Hoyle, sir.'

'Mr Hoyle, now?' Near-contempt was in the question.

'He bullied him, sir. Wouldn't even allow him to speak.'

From behind Clarke the motor patrol sergeant growled, 'Amen to that.'

'Sergeant?' Flensing moved his head slightly and looked at the motor patrol sergeant.

The motor patrol sergeant rose to his feet and joined Clarke at the desk.

'You agree with Constable Clarke?' purred Flensing.

'I do, sir.'

'That Wardman was subject to – er – shall we say harassment?'

'Serious harassment, sir.'

'Physical? Verbal?'

'Both, as far as Belamy was concerned.' The motor patrol sergeant, having shown his hand, plunged in with what he believed to be the truth. 'Belamy thumped him about the face.'

'In the car?'

'No, sir. When we stopped for a meal. When Wardman went to the toilet.'

'The – er – toilet, sergeant.'

'When he tried to escape from custody,' contributed Hoyle softly.

Flensing breathed, 'Aahh!'

'He'd been caught,' rumbled the motor patrol sergeant. 'He was back in custody. There was no need to lay a finger on him.'

Flensing remained silent for a moment, then he looked directly at the motor patrol sergeant and asked, 'What opinion do you hold as far as homosexuals are concerned, sergeant?'

'They should be allowed to live their own lives.'

'Clarke?' Flensing turned his head a little.

'The same, sir. They shouldn't be hounded.'

Very gently – very pointedly – Flensing said, 'Clive Richardson was a homosexual.' He allowed the pause to give the words enough time to register, then added, 'He wasn't allowed to live his own life. He wasn't even allowed to *live*.'

'Sir, we're not talking about . . .'

'I know exactly what you're talking about, sergeant.' The drawling quality left Flensing's voice. It was suddenly replaced by hard, whiplash rank. 'You're championing a murderer. Both of you. You're forgetting a man battered to death in his own home. *I'm not*!

'You – Clarke – you've seen fit to make the first complaint. That a detective sergeant isn't taking a statement as *you'd* like him to take it. You . . . a beat constable. Standing in judgement on an experienced C.I.D. sergeant. In effect, the substance of your complaint – a murderer isn't getting justice. That's *your* opinion. Not mine. Let me remind you, Clarke. Justice. It also means punishing the wrongdoer. The innocent have nothing to fear. Equally, the guilty get what they deserve.

'We need that statement. It isn't *vital* – we have enough evidence to stand Wardman in a dock with a ninety per-cent certainty of a conviction – I want a hundred per-cent certainty. Therefore, I want that statement. Sergeant Belamy knows this. Sergeant Belamy will *get* me that statement . . . with or without you as witness. He'll do it his way, and justice will be done.'

Flensing turned his attention to the motor patrol sergeant.

'You, sergeant. Your job is to drive motor cars, not criticise senior detective officers. Tell me – for the record – how many murder enquiries have *you* conducted?'

'None, sir.' The motor patrol sergeant stiffened as Flensing's implied insult slammed home.

'But you know how it should be done? It comes naturally to you? You took it in at your mother's breast?' The withering sarcasm was taken over by a red-hot blistering. 'Sergeant, for your information, I do not take note of criticism of a senior C.I.D. officer when that criticism comes from a lower-ranker whose forte is driving motor cars. Wardman is guilty . . . understand that and never forget that. And you, and this misguided constable, have the audacity – the blind stupidity – to champion a murderer against the police. Against your own kind.

'If there was any doubt – even the shadow of a doubt – I might try to understand. But no! You set yourself up as judge and jury. Both of you.' He glanced at the white-faced Clarke. 'You've decided. You know little or nothing about the mass of evidence against Wardman, and yet you've decided. He hasn't had "a fair crack of the whip", to use the puerile expression favoured by Clarke. What about Richardson? Or doesn't he matter?'

'He matters, sir.' The voice of the motor patrol sergeant was tight with suppressed rage.

'I doubt it,' snapped Flensing. 'Not the way you two

168

argue. A man has his head smashed to pulp . . . and for no good reason. But you two concern yourself with the animal responsible. You argue *his* cause. *He* mustn't be inconvenienced. *He* mustn't be made to feel uncomfortable. What the hell sort of logic is that, sergeant? What the hell sort of *policing* is that?'

'Good policing.' The motor patrol sergeant began to fight back.

'*Good policing!*'

'He's innocent until . . .'

'Sergeant, don't quote textbook law to me. Don't set yourself up on a pedestal and tell *me* the do's and don'ts, as itemised by academic lunatics who wouldn't know how to start detecting major crime. *Guilty.* Guilty as hell. That's what the evidence says, and there's too much evidence to leave the slightest doubt. He goes where he's meant to go. How he gets there is of no importance.'

'Of no . . .'

'Of no importance whatever. If he has to be "fixed" he *gets* "fixed". In Wardman's case it needs very little fixing . . . but what it needs it will get with my full approval.'

'You're mad!' exploded the motor patrol sergeant. 'Stark staring bloody mad. You're a copper like the rest of us. Not judge, jury, executioner . . . everything. You can't just . . .'

'I damn well *can*. I *will*. Wardman's a murderer, sergeant. The ultimate rogue of the human species . . .'

'. . . commit perjury, just for the sake of never being wrong. That blasted rank you carry doesn't entitle you to do *that*.'

'. . . and he'll pay. He'll pay in full. That I promise you. As for perjury. Get your priorities right, man. What's perjury compared with murder? A small wrong to right the largest wrong of all. Good God, you don't think I'd hesitate, if I thought for a moment . . .'

'He's innocent.' It came on a breath of expelled air; as if

169

the pressure had increased to a point beyond which Clarke could no longer control it. He almost sighed, 'Dear Christ, he's innocent . . . I killed Richardson. Not Wardman. *I killed him.*'

NINE

There was a silence. There *had* to be a silence; a long silence; a silence which seemed to be charged with static electricity. A police officer had confessed to committing murder in the presence of four of his colleagues. And it *was* a confession. The tone of voice, the almost shouted words, the passion with which those words had been spoken. Nothing empty. Nothing wild and ridiculous. Richardson had been battered to death, and the man responsible was accepting his responsibility . . . no qualifications.

Flensing dropped his act, and in a gentler voice said, 'Get him a chair please, Mr Hoyle.'

Hoyle rose, carried a chair to the desk and slowly – as if he'd suddenly aged – Clarke lowered himself and sat with his hands clasping his kneecaps. Pale, but in some strange way with a look of relief on his face. As if a great burden had been lifted from him.

Flensing nodded, and the motor patrol sergeant returned to *his* chair and sat down.

Shaw gaped, open-mouthed. He realised he was in on something almost unique . . . and it scared him a little.

Flensing said, 'Constable. Take your time. Say what you wish to say, but know you needn't say anything.'

'It – it has to be told, sir,' whispered Clarke.

'For Wardman's sake?'

Clarke nodded.

'In that case, know you're with people who will try to

171

understand,' Flensing told him.

'Yes, sir. Thank you, sir.'

It was a simple story told in simple but halting words. No excuses. No involved explanations. And, above all else, the truth, recognised by both Flensing and Hoyle *as* the truth.

'I'm a homosexual, sir. I tried to fight it. Up to joining the force – *after* I'd joined the force – I tried to fight it. Tried to be what you would call "normal". I – I couldn't. I failed. I even tried to get a girl friend. I couldn't. I could be friends . . . be *her* friend. But no more than that. The – the thought of . . .'

He halted and lowered his head, not able to find the right words.

'Clarke.' Flensing's voice was quiet and paternal. He leaned forward a little as he spoke. 'Clarke, I think common sense suggests that words such as "normal", "abnormal", "perversion" – those sort of words – are unnecessary. You refuse to allow an innocent person to stand accused of a crime you committed. That, to me, is the only thing of real importance. That of itself makes you a man . . . a *complete* man.'

'Thank you, sir.' Clarke raised his head and continued his story. 'A homosexual, you see, sir. *And* a police officer. I thought it could work. Perhaps it can. Maybe there *are* homosexual policemen. I don't see why not. I don't see why they can't be *good* policemen.'

'Nor do I,' murmured Flensing.

'But – but better than me, sir. Wiser than me.' He moistened his lips, then drew the back of a hand across his mouth. 'I – I wanted to keep it a secret. I was ashamed of . . . No, sir. I *wasn't* ashamed. I'd grown past that stage. But I was frightened. Frightened of being asked to resign. I think . . .' He shook his head sadly. 'I think – with respect, sir – I think the force should make it known. The official attitude to men like me. As long as they do their job. As long as they don't disgrace the service. I – I think it should be *known*, sir.'

'I'm – er – inclined to agree. It's time a decision *was* made.'

'Yes, sir. That's why . . .' He cleared his throat before continuing. 'I – er – learned of the others, of course. The other homosexuals. Some of them. Most of them, I think. It's part of the job . . . to *know* them. I wanted to become one of them. Openly, I mean. To be accepted as one of them. Without shame. Without secrecy. I suppose – I *think* – I wanted a companion. *One* companion. Like man and wife. That sort of relationship. Somebody I could trust. Set up home together. Be what we were and *still* be a policeman.

'It wasn't possible, of course. A dream, really. I daren't even approach anybody. That's – that's why I fell in with Richardson. Not because I liked him particularly. I certainly didn't *love* him. I mean, nobody could love a man like Richardson . . .'

'He's probably been taken short,' grunted Belamy. 'We don't really *need* him. It's me you're making the statement to, sonny. Now, you bashed him over the head. How many times?'

'I – er – I don't know.'

'Come on!'

'I can't remember,' insisted Wardman.

'Just kept belting, that it?'

'Er – yes – I suppose so.'

'Right.' Belamy poised the ballpoint once more. '"I hit him over the head a lot of times. I don't know how many. Even when he was dead, I kept on hitting him." That about sum it up?'

'It's one way of putting it,' sighed Wardman.

'Aye, well, no need to be coy now, sonny. It's what you did. It might as well go down.'

173

'Richardson was a . . .' Clarke stopped for a moment, took a deep breath, then continued, 'He's dead. He can't defend himself. But if you ask around. Make enquiries.' The quick, twisted smile held only sadness. 'We're like women, aren't we? That's what it boils down to. Good wives and whores. We're like *that*, except we're men. Richardson was a whore. A whore of *our* kind.

'I went with him, because . . . it was *necessary*. I needed . . . Oh, Christ, how can I explain it to anybody? Who'll understand. I should have had more control. I should have . . .'

'You went with Richardson,' interrupted Flensing soothingly. 'Men go with loose women. You went with Richardson. Same thing. We *do* understand.'

'Thank you, sir.' Clarke remained silent for a moment. He seemed to gather himself, as if getting his emotional second-wind. 'I visited him, you see, sir. Not often. Not regularly. Just – just occasionally. He – er – he knew I was a policeman. At first I tried to keep it from him, but he met me once on duty. In uniform.

'I was scared. Terrified. Y'see – as I've said – I didn't *know*. And – and if he told anybody . . . Anyway he didn't and – and it seemed all right. I'd – I'd call in. Sometimes – not often but sometimes – when I was on duty. Near where he lived, you see. Not always for . . . sex. Sometimes just to talk. I – er – I even made enquiries. Some of the small crimes. He seemed to know most people and he might have been able to help. He – er – couldn't, or didn't.

'Then – then the last time I called. The night he died. The night I killed him. He – he offered me what he called a "joint". A cigarette. Pot. Cannabis. Dammit, I was on duty, and he offered me that . . .'

'What did you use to bash his brains out with?' asked Belamy bluntly.

174

'I keep telling you', muttered Wardman. 'I don't *know.*'

'Of course you bloody well know. What did you do it with?'

'I don't *know.*'

'If I put down here . . .' Belamy motioned towards the statement forms. 'If I put down here, "I refuse to tell the police what the murder weapon was or what I did with it" that'll *really* look bad. No co-operation worth a damn. No . . .'

'Can we wait until the constable gets back?' pleaded Wardman.

'Clarke?' Belamy glared. 'We don't need Clarke. Christ Almighty, man! You're in the fertiliser. Up to the eyeballs in it. What the hell good is Clarke going to do?'

'Dope, you see, sir, dope.' Clarke removed his hands from his knees, clasped his fingers together, leaned forward a little and rested the clasped hands on the front edge of Flensing's desk. Gradually, he had become more composed. Gradually, he was realising that this detective chief superintendent wasn't seeking anything other than the truth. Clarke continued, 'He wasn't big. I'm not suggesting that. Just that he used the stuff. Smoked these joints. I don't know where he got them . . . I didn't ask. But I asked him whether he'd offered them to other people, and he said he had. To kids. To youngsters looking for kicks.

'He – he wasn't *big.*' Clarke unclasped then re-clasped his fingers. 'I don't think he was a pusher. Not even as big as that. But he *did* sell some of those joint things to kids. He – he admitted it. He even thought it was funny. He laughed when he made the admission. And – y'know – glue sniffing, dope, that sort of thing. It's – it's what the argument was about. The argument that ended up by my killing him.'

In the pause, Flensing said, 'I should remind you of the Official Caution, Clarke. You know it, of course.'

'Yes, sir.'

'Just to remind you, that's all. It applies to you no less

than to anybody else.'

'I'll not hide behind it, sir.' The quick smile was sad, but in some strange way not without dignity. He continued, 'What we did, sir. There's a small room – a dressing-room – off the bedroom. Richardson was wearing a dressing-gown when I arrived. That's all he was wearing. I undressed in the small room, and joined him in the bedroom.

'Then – after we'd finished, after he'd offered me the joint – we had this argument. I – I went a bit far, I suppose. Silly, really. I threatened to arrest him. The kids, you see. I didn't care about *him*, but the kids . . . It – it turned him nasty. He said he'd ruin me. Get me kicked out of the force. Oh, I don't know, arguments – they start at nothing then wind up into a real storm. It shouldn't have done, but it did. It – it lasted, too. Must have. I know he'd finished the joint and thrown the ash away, and the row was getting worse and worse all the time. We were swearing at each other. Threatening each other. Calling each other names . . .'

'Sonny.' Belamy's voice was lowering itself into a threatening snarl. 'Sonny, if you think you're going to walk away from a murder rap by being smart-arse with *me*, you've picked the wrong man.'

'No. I'm not being . . .'

'Of course you know what you bloody well hit him with.'

'I don't. I swear . . .'

'You've read all that cock about "Motive", "Means" and "Opportunity" . . . right. You think you have us all by the short and curlies just because we can't find the sodding weapon.'

'No. It's not that. It's just . . .'

'Well, let me tell you, sonny. That bloody weapon is going to be *named*. It's going to be *found*. And you're going to name it and say where it can be found in this damn statement . . . get it? Over your miserable signature, you

176

disgusting queer.'

Wardman blinked, touched his lips with his fingers, then whispered, 'Not unless the constable's here.'

'What?' Belamy's eyes popped a little.

'The constable. I'll only sign the statement if the constable's here.'

'You mean *Clarke*?'

'I think he should be . . .'

'Clarke is a nothing,' bawled Belamy. 'Clarke is a bloody wooden-top. A door-knob-twister. *I'm* Jack-the-Lad as far as you're concerned, sonny, not Clarke. It's what *I* say that matters.'

'I – I think we went a little mad. I'm sure. Both of us. I – I don't expect other people to understand, but . . . What we'd just done. There *is* shame y'know, sir. With me there is. There shouldn't be, I know. With other gays there isn't. The good ones. The honest ones. They know – *I* know – it's our way of life. Different to the so-called "straight" way, but no worse. But – but with me the shame is still there. That, and the dope, and giving it to kids, and his threatening to get me kicked out of the force . . . things got out of hand.'

There was a slight pause. Clarke looked at Flensing's face, but saw neither disgust nor approval. Merely patience and an attempt at understanding. Clarke continued, 'That's when it happened, sir.'

'When you killed him?' said Flensing, gently.

Clarke nodded, then said, 'I'd left my clothes – I've already told you . . . the adjoining room. I went in there and got my truncheon. That's what I killed him with. Over the head. God knows how many times.' Then, in a whisper, 'Once I'd started, I couldn't *stop!*'

He moved in the chair, slipped a police truncheon from its pocket down the right side of his trousers and placed the truncheon carefully on the desk top. He hesitated, then felt in his hip pocket and placed handcuffs alongside the truncheon.

He said, 'I'm sorry, sir. I haven't my warrant card with me.'

'That the one?' Flensing nodded at the truncheon.

'No, sir. I burned it. It was – y'know – covered in blood. That's one I took from the changing room. Belonging to one of the other men. I don't know who. He'll – he'll have missed it.'

'He'll have indented for a new truncheon. That what you mean?'

Clarke nodded.

'We'll check. Go on.'

'Well, that's it, sir. It wasn't Wardman. Me. I showered the mess off, dressed, then left. That's all. It wasn't Wardman. Wardman's just – y'know – scared. What he saw later. But it wasn't *him*.'

The confession ended with sudden abruptness. Finished. Done. Told. Thereafter, silence. A thick, almost solid silence which was more than a mere absence of sound. Clarke was trembling a little, breathing slightly quicker than usual . . . as if he'd just ended an exhausting race.

Flensing murmured, 'A statement?'

'It's necessary, sir. To get Wardman off the hook.'

'Of course.'

'But not by Belamy. I'll not have . . .'

'Not Belamy,' soothed Flensing. 'Chief Inspector Hoyle?'

Clarke hesitated, then said, 'I write it myself.'

'Certainly.'

'No prompting. No putting words into my mouth.'

'Every word your own handwriting,' promised Flensing.

'The chief inspector just as a witness. Nothing more.'

'Include him as such in the statement, if that's what you want.'

Clarke nodded.

'Anything else?'

Clarke moved his head. He stared, first at Hoyle, then at Shaw, then at the motor patrol sergeant. Hoyle and Shaw lowered their eyes. The motor patrol sergeant met the gaze and held it. Clarke turned to Flensing again, tried to speak, failed, then tried again. It came out as little more than a croak.

'I'm – I'm sorry, sir. About the force. I'm sorry I've . . .'

His head lowered, he raised his hands to cover his face, and the tears came.

'Shaw.'

'Sir.'

'Take him to Number Two Interview Room.' The tone was gentle enough to make it sound like a request. 'Sit with him. Allow him to compose himself. Mr Hoyle will be along presently.'

'Yes, sir.' Shaw rose from his chair.

'And Shaw. Call at Number One Interview Room. Tell Sergeant Belamy and Wardman to come to this office . . . and to bring all statements and documents with them.'

'Yes, sir.'

Three women slept or napped. It was a time for sleep and, after an emotionally draining day, it had been impossible to stay away from sleep.

Helen Flensing rested her head sideways on the pillow. Her heavy breathing almost amounted to a genteel snore and a trickle of saliva ran from the corner of her open mouth and dampened the material upon which she rested her head.

And as she slept, she dreamed. Of the west coast, long stretches of beaches, unpolluted waves in which she and a detective sergeant splashed and swam and paddled. Of high blue skies, shrieking seagulls diving for thrown bread and a newly-married couple racing each other across wet sand. Of laughter and kisses and love-making – such love-making – in secret hollows of sandhills . . . and all this

179

for ever and ever.

Jean Belamy slept in the armchair, with her feet still tucked under her and her head forward with her chin on her chest. It was a shallow sleep – part-sleep, part-doze – yet she too dreamed. Dreamed and remembered. Remembered . . . perhaps even regretted a little. Arguments, squabbles, stupidities. He was her man, but he could also have been her child. She'd mistaken arrogance for strength of character. Bigotry for experience. Dogmatism for wisdom. She wasn't the first . . . she wouldn't be the last. He could have been changed. The right woman – a stronger woman – and he could have been changed. Made into a nicer person. A more complete man. She could have made him the child they'd never had . . . a substitute child without him knowing it. Shown him the way. Forced him into reasonableness. Insisted that *she* was of more importance than his job.

What then? What then?

What a different life. What a pleasanter life. What tranquillity. But never for her . . . never for them.

Alva, too, slept. On a not-too-comfortable chair, her arms folded on a bedside table, she was leaning forward with her cheek resting on her forearms . . . dreaming.

Wales. The wild valleys of her youth, the wild blood of her youth and a man – a complete stranger – holding her and loving her as only a Welshman could. No David, this stranger. No white-skinned, simpering Englishman. No gentle, timid love-making. The wild way, the Welsh way. The *real* way. Black hair flying, white teeth gleaming, dark skin glistening with carnal sweat. A coupling of animal savagery and, in the background – beyond the hills – the sound of men's voices in song. Some monumental male voice choir, roaring and softening as only Welsh choirs can. A minor key carrying the Welsh language as an accompaniment to Welsh love-making . . . and never would be and never *could* be.

180

But what a dream! What a might-have-been!

Hoyle had replaced the chair. The motor patrol officer was back, seated and more or less relaxed. On the desk, alongside the truncheon and handcuffs, was a small pile of statement forms and the folder holding the file of the Richardson enquiry. Wardman had taken the seat previously used by Clarke; Belamy had at first made token objection, but Flensing had said, 'Let him sit down, sergeant,' and Belamy had grudgingly complied. Belamy was also seated. His chair was that which had been used by Detective Constable Shaw.

It was a little like a seminar, with Flensing holding the place of chairman. A waiting. A tension. An anxiety to get under way.

Flensing lighted a cigarette, pulled an ash-tray an inch or so nearer, then in his normal, controlled drawl spoke.

'A murder enquiry, gentlemen. All of you part of it.' He gave a tiny, nodding smile at the motor patrol sergeant. 'Even you, sergeant, part of it. To know who the murderer is. To have sufficient evidence to *know*, but insufficient evidence to hope for a conviction.' He sighed. It was a stage-sigh; an underlining of his words. 'It happens, gentlemen. It happens far more often than the general public realise. Lesser crime? It annoys, but we can wait. Lesser crime is repeated and, hopefully, *next* time the criminal will make an even bigger mistake. More evidence. The certainty of a conviction.'

He drew on the cigarette, then continued, 'Not so with murder. A man commits murder . . . period. The chances of his *again* committing murder are slim. Therefore just the once. If the man we're after is "A" – if after studying every ounce of evidence at our disposal, we are convinced it is "A" – then "A" must be brought to justice . . . within the law, of course.'

'And has been.' As Flensing paused, Belamy spoke. He

181

jerked his head in the direction of Wardman and continued, 'He's coughed. It's all there in the statement.'

The motor patrol sergeant cleared his throat, seemed about to say something, but remained silent.

'The – er – statement,' murmured Flensing.

'It's all in there, sir.'

Very gently Flensing said, 'Constable Clarke has suggested that the statement is more *your* statement than it is Wardman's.'

'With respect, sir . . .'

'Don't!' Flensing smiled. 'Those three words are invariably the prelude to something *dis*respectful. Just say what you have to say, sergeant. Don't spoil things by hedging your bets.'

'Clarke doesn't know what the devil he's talking about,' said Belamy bluntly.

'An opinion,' nodded Flensing.

'It needed saying.'

'And has been said.' Flensing turned his attention to Hoyle, and continued, 'The chief inspector. Originally it was his idea. I think he should take up the story.'

'Thank you, sir.' Hoyle moistened his lips. 'Evidence, but not *enough* evidence. That's what we were faced with. We needed a statement. More than that we needed a Guilty plea . . . with as little a chance as possible that that plea might be changed in court.'

'It won't be changed, sir,' promised Belamy.

'For Christ's sake!' hissed the motor patrol sergeant.

Hoyle smiled at Wardman and in a strangely gentle tone, said, 'Did you make a statement, Mr Wardman?'

'Sergeant Belamy wrote words down,' said Wardman flatly.

'Your words?'

'*His* words. His interpretation of what I *should* . . .'

'That's a damn lie!'

'Belamy.' The motor patrol sergeant could contain

182

himself no longer. 'Can't you see they're giving you rope? You've hung your stupid self already. For God's sake, don't . . .'

'Murderers.' Hoyle raised his voice high enough to successfully interrupt the interchange. Then in a lower voice, he continued, 'Murderers are not all evil men. Some are of course. It would be silly to suggest otherwise. But not all. Some are weak. Some are driven to it. Some commit murder on the spur of the moment, and regret it for the rest of their lives.

'And some,' continued Hoyle softly, 'know enough about law – about the Criminal Law – to know that it needs an uncommon amount of concrete *and* circumstantial evidence to hope for a conviction.' This time the pause was allowed to run its few moments without interruption. 'We had evidence, then. But not enough evidence. Nevertheless, evidence sufficient to convince us that the person Mr Flensing has seen fit to refer to as "A" was our man . . . and our man knew the law. "A" knew we'd hit a brick wall. We'd unearthed everything we *could* unearth, and he was still free. He hadn't even been interviewed. His name was known, but only to three members of this force. The chief constable, because he *had* to know, Detective Chief Superintendent Flensing and myself. The file – the *real* file – was kept under strict wraps.'

'The *real* file?' growled Belamy.

'The file that showed the fingerprints, but without enough points of comparison to allow them to be produced as evidence. The file that showed the times – the opportunity – but those times could apply to other people, too. The motive, we didn't know. We guessed, and were half-right. Richardson, and the sort of man he was, and the murderer – and the man *he* was – gave pointers. Good pointers. But there were things we didn't know.'

'Dope,' muttered the motor patrol sergeant.

'What dope?' Belamy looked puzzled.

183

'Cunning was called for.' Hoyle smiled and ignored both the motor patrol sergeant and Belamy. 'An assessment of the character of the murderer.' Then he spoke directly to Belamy and purred, 'A murderer with a conscience, sergeant? Is it possible?'

'I'd say not.'

'Fixed ideas.'

'Eh?'

'You. You have very fixed ideas.'

'I know right from wrong.'

'That makes you a clever man, sergeant. It's more than I know.'

'Fancy talk, sir.' Contempt touched his eyes. 'I'm a copper. I don't waste time worrying about reasons. Digging for possible reasons.'

'And homosexuals?' asked Hoyle gently.

'Queers? It's their choice. If they want perversion, let 'em get on with it.'

'All cut and dried, right?'

'It makes me a good copper.'

'*Wrong*.' Hoyle's tone hardened. 'That's why you were chosen, sergeant. You lived up to every expectation.'

'That statement.' Belamy pointed. 'It nails *that* queer.' The finger was exchanged for a thumb, and the thumb jerked in the direction of Wardman. '*He* knows the strength of it. You had him. In the car, you had him. But I'd softened him up. And along there in Number One Interview Room I made bloody sure . . .'

His voice trailed off into silence as Flensing picked the statement forms from his desk and slowly, deliberately, tore them into two halves then dropped them into the waste-paper basket.

Wardman chuckled quietly and said, 'Some statement.'

'Look, sonny, if you think . . .'

'Sit down, sergeant, and shut up.' Flensing took over from Hoyle. He lifted the file from the desk top, tore that also and dropped it into the basket with the statement.

Flensing said, 'We'll put you out of your misery, Sergeant Belamy.' Then to Hoyle, 'I'll take over, David.'

'Yes, sir.' Hoyle nodded.

'Know your man.' Flensing bent and slipped a foldered file from one of the desk drawers. He placed it in front of him, then continued, 'Or, to be precise, know your *men*.

'You, Belamy. The perfect red-necked cop. The bully-boy. That's why *you* travelled to the south coast and back. To give the murderer hell. The sort of hell only your kind are capable of giving. What *you* think is good policing. You, sergeant,' he turned his attention to the motor patrol sergeant. 'Somebody capable of driving from here to the south coast and back in a day. Doing it with moderate speed and as much safety as possible . . . and with a minimum amount of relief at the wheel. Chief Inspector Hoyle couldn't spell you too much. He had other things to do. To keep the con moving in the right direction, among other things.'

'The con?' growled Belamy.

'One huge con, sergeant.' Flensing smiled with his lips, but allowed a chill to touch his eyes and reach his tone. 'You were the big wheel. Your – er – so-called "style". Without it, it wouldn't have come off.'

'Sir, I made Wardman . . .'

'Detective Inspector Wardman, sergeant. The time is ripe to grant him full style and title.'

Belamy opened and closed his mouth, like a stranded fish.

'You see,' continued Flensing, 'we didn't *quite* have Clarke.'

'Clarke?' whispered Belamy.

'Police Constable Clarke . . . the man handcuffed to Inspector Wardman. Every time you spoke to the inspector you were, in effect, talking to Clarke. Clarke knew it. You didn't.'

185

'But . . .' The motor patrol sergeant recovered from the shock of the news. 'He escaped custody. He tried to make a run for it.'

Wardman said, 'To build up a case against myself, sergeant. To help a little.'

'It *can't* be Clarke,' said Belamy.

'It *is* Clarke.' Flensing tapped the file he'd taken from the desk drawer. 'We've almost enough here . . . almost but not quite. We have enough *now*. He's confessed. Everything. He's waiting to make a statement.'

'In that case, why the hell . . .'

'Cool down, Belamy.' Hoyle interrupted. 'Something you'll never understand. Clarke has a conscience. He truly thought another man was going down for a crime he'd committed. He couldn't let that happen.'

'*I've* been conned,' rasped Belamy.

'You have, indeed.' Flensing nodded. 'Chief Inspector Hoyle's idea. As I've already said – the red-necked approach – we used it.'

'And – and – and . . .' Belamy choked on the words. 'That file, that file I was waving around in the car, that file I . . .'

'The file I tore up?' smiled Flensing.

'It – it was all *balls*? It was . . .'

'It was the file as we'd have *liked* it to have been. Let's put it that way. Complete fingerprints where, in fact, we only have part-fingerprints – useless in court. Statements that were never made. A doctored file. Doctored for a purpose.'

'To – to make me look a complete idiot.'

'No.' Flensing shook his head. 'To make you act a part.'

'To make you act yourself,' growled Hoyle.

'*You* didn't do so damn bad!' exploded Belamy.

'Ah, but I knew,' said Hoyle. 'Inspector Wardman knew. Just the two of us. What *I* did – what *he* did – was for the benefit of Clarke. The difference, you see, sergeant. You

186

worked to make Inspector Wardman crack. Inspector Wardman and I worked to make Clarke crack.'

'I'm going home.' The motor patrol sergeant rose from his chair. His face reflected his general disgust. 'I have a bed waiting. I need sleep.' He paused, then added, 'I also need a hot bath, if only to get the foulness of today scrubbed off.'

'We've detected a murder, sergeant.' Flensing pulled rank. Gently, but certainly. 'There's also one last order. It applies to all of you. Silence. Absolute silence about the activities of today. Clarke will be kept incommunicado. Absolutely. Apart from a solicitor – who will be told only what Clarke can tell him – he will see nobody. You may like the man.' Flensing gave a quick nod of understanding. 'You may even think he's had a rough deal. You're entitled to that opinion, as long as you keep it to yourself. As long as you *also* remember that, as a serving police officer, he committed the crime of murder.' He looked hard at the motor patrol sergeant. 'Clear, sergeant?'

'Quite clear, sir.'

The motor patrol sergeant walked, stiff-legged, from the office. He closed the door gently, but very deliberately, as he left.

And now Belamy stood by the desk facing Flensing. Oddly, there was an unusual but furious dignity about the man. He spoke in a low voice – little more than a growl – but, despite the hint of a tremor occasionally, it was controlled.

He said, 'I'm not pleased, sir.'

'I didn't expect you to be, sergeant.' The hardness of Flensing's tone matched Belamy's.

'I don't like being made into a monkey.'

'Not a monkey. A gorilla. That's what we needed.'

'Channels of complaint?' said Belamy tightly.

'What channels? What complaint? You did what comes naturally.'

187

'I was used.'

'Of course.' Flensing nodded briefly.

'I'll not be used again.'

'True.' Flensing lifted the flap of the file and slid out an already completed form. As he pushed it towards Belamy he said, 'You're off the streets, sergeant. Administration in Fingerprint Section. Filing prints . . . *not* visiting scenes of crime. You start Monday at nine. Till then you're on leave.'

Belamy stared at the form for a moment then, as he picked it up, he grated, 'Big deal.'

From behind Belamy Wardman murmured, 'Try thumping Fingerprint Forms.'

Belamy spun round, took a step which brought him face-to-face with Wardman. Pent-up fury and frustration made his voice and expression ugly.

'Wardman. *Inspector* Wardman . . . what the hell your name is. I thumped you. Sure I thumped you. I should have broken your bloody neck.'

Without another word he strode from the office. They watched him, but said nothing.

Flensing gave a wry smile, then mused, 'We're getting more unpopular by the minute.'

Whisky and cigarettes were out and the three men were seated in an irregular pattern around Flensing's desk. It had come off; the gamble had worked and a murder had been detected. But nobody was throwing hats in the air with glee.

'You did a fine job.' Hoyle congratulated Wardman. 'That "escape" stunt was a masterpiece.'

'Yeah.' Wardman touched his swollen and discoloured face. 'It was necessary. The pile-up broke the concentration. Something had to be done to bring the trolley back onto the tracks.'

'Belamy can be very physical.'

'Obviously.'

'I'll send a confidential report to your chief,' promised Flensing.

'He *might* have cracked,' volunteered Wardman. 'Good interrogation – real interrogation, not Belamy-style – he *might* have buckled. He's weak . . . not bad.'

'He's a copper,' sighed Flensing. 'Or *was*. Kidology wouldn't have worked. He knew enough to keep his mouth shut and stay safe.'

'Maybe.'

'It is a great pity,' continued Flensing, 'that it all has to be kept under wraps.' He tasted whisky and drew on the cigarette. 'Those lunatics who yell for some sort of quango organisation to police the police. Only *we* could have pulled it. Policemen.'

'Cunning bastards.' Hoyle's observation was shot with mild disgust.

'If necessary.' Flensing smiled. 'Or would you rather have a murderer in the force?'

'It was necessary,' agreed Hoyle gruffly.

'There's a bed waiting for you.' Flensing spoke to Wardman. 'Bed and an English breakfast. At the Plymouth Sound Hotel. Strangely enough, Clarke's favourite drinking spot . . . so I'm told.'

'The Plymouth Sound?' Wardman seemed slightly surprised.

'We have a Turk's Head,' smiled Hoyle. 'Nothing to do with Turkey, I'm afraid. Somebody comes up with these names.'

'Even a Snowdonia,' added Flensing. Then, 'You'll find a first class rail ticket back home with the night porter.'

'Thanks.'

'Thank *you*.'

'What about the face?' asked Hoyle.

'Scars of battle.' Wardman stood up from the chair and, at the same time, finished off his drink. 'I'll get to the hotel. Get it bathed. It looks worse than it is.'

189

Flensing reached for the desk phone, 'Again . . . thanks. I'll get a squad car to drive you to the hotel.'

Jean Belamy stood in the kitchen of their home and waited for the coffee to percolate. She stood with stiffened arms and hands resting on the edge of the Formica-topped working surface. She stood with her head bowed . . . but happy.

Supremely – stupidly – happy.

The raving, the language, the blind fury didn't mean a thing. It would go. It would die. Then he'd be back. The man she'd married. The gruff, biased fool to whom everything was either black or white – right or wrong – with no room between for grey areas. But *hers*.

Nine-to-five days. Every day. Office hours with every weekend free. Oh, he'd hate it at first. Detest it. But he'd grow used to it. Accept it. Then they'd have a life together . . . a *real* life. A life not bounded by the movement of evil men. Not limited to a few hours each week when Dick wasn't fighting what he'd come to see as a personal war.

He'd mellow a little. Of course he would. Oh, he'd never become smarmy or smooth-tongued. He never had been and never would be. But the basic decency – the basic honesty – which she'd once known hadn't gone for ever. It *couldn't* have gone for ever. He'd change back to his old self. Slowly. Perhaps very slowly. But surely.

The tears pricked the back of her eyes. Tears of happiness. Tears of relief.

Flensing and Hoyle screwed their cigarettes out in the large glass ash-tray on Flensing's desk.

Flensing said, 'You've had a long day, David.'

'It's not over yet.' Hoyle touched his mouth with a hand to kill a yawn. 'That statement needs taking.'

'Easy with him,' said Flensing gently.

'I – er – I have a certain reputation to retrieve.'

190

'He's suffered.' Flensing's voice was sad. 'Not Wardman. Wardman knew he was innocent. But Clarke knew *he* was guilty – he took everything thrown at Wardman – and couldn't answer back. Softly on the homosexual thing.'

'Of course.'

'And tell him. Make him realise. We can't be on his side, can't go as far as that . . . but we honour him.'

The night sister opened the door gently, looked in, then closed the door.

She led Flensing a few yards away from the door, then said, 'They're both sleeping.'

'Leave them,' sighed Flensing. 'Alva's husband won't be off duty for a couple of hours. That, at least. I'll be in later to see Helen.'

'They think a lot of each other,' observed the night sister.

'Uhu.' Flensing nodded. 'Two fine women.'

'Each with a good husband.'

'For what we are,' agreed Flensing sadly. 'We do our best. But – y'see – our job boils down to destruction. At best we're "necessary".'

'You look tired, chief superintendent.'

'Very tired.'

'I have some freshly-made tea in my office. There's also an empty side-ward with a bed ready for somebody to sleep in. It would save the journey home . . . and the journey back.'

'That,' said Flensing gently, 'would be appreciated. Both. Very much appreciated.'